White Window

Koushik Roy

First published in India 2010
Apodis Indica
Imprint of Fortytwo Bookz Galaxy
3/21 Anand Nagar
Opp Bilwara Bhavan
Santacruz (E)
Mumbai 400055

ISBN No. : 978-81-908411-6-0

Cover Design : Gajanan Adhav
Typeset in Book Antique
Printed at Surekha Press, Mumbai

Price – India : Rs195; Elsewhere: US $9

Koushik Roy is a freelance writer. He has Masters in Journalism and English Literature. He travels extensively for writing. His short story "Suitcase" was published in Indian Voices, Vol.-I. His second novel "Still the Blue Dove Sings"is under the consideration of a leading UK literary agency.

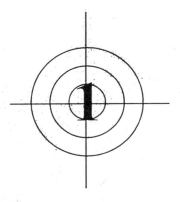

Nicholas Gorskov hated waiting in a seedy hotel room. The captain of a cargo ship owned by an Arab tycoon, this Latvian respected time and was a disciplined person. But he also knew where to make a quick buck and valued the additional income that could help his love for the good things in life. The illegal aspect of making money didn't bother him much. The lure of dollars also allowed him to ignore the fact that the person who was supposed to meet him in this hotel room in Brussels was already two hours late.

Belgium is, according to the security experts, an easy gateway between France and Northern Europe; maybe for this reason it has attracted many international criminals. Brussels is at the crossroads of Europe and crimes like drugs and human trafficking, prostitution, passport fraud, and illegal arms deal thrive here. The problem is deep- rooted and one of the causes might be the multi-ethnic character of the city.

A walk along the streets around the Gare du Midi in Brussels leaves one in no doubt that the place is a hotspot for criminal activities. The bars, restaurants and hotels have a shady look around them and are populated with an assortment of people like East- Europeans, Arabs, former KGB spies, Africans, Afghans, and Pakistanis. Curiously the locality's main street has earned the nickname "Kandahar Lane".

According to the FBI, the premier investigating agency of the US, it was here that Richard Reid, the accused "shoe bomber," stayed several days in a hotel making a special blueprint to blow up an American Airlines jet. The nearby Marrakech was an Internet cafe where Reid possibly made an appointment with other terrorists to collect the explosives.

Another restaurant was Le Nil, where Belgian police officers raided to unearth chemicals that had supposedly been stacked there by members of a Tunisian network linked to Al Qaeda. The FBI had sufficient clues to believe that the chemicals that the police could seize - 220 pounds of sulfur and 16 gallons of acetone - Reid tried to use to make a deadly bomb to blow up the US Embassy in Paris.

The sharp knock on the door woke Nicholas up from the light nap he had drifted into. "Who is it?" he asked.

"I have the consignment for India," a husky voice answered.

The name of the country was sufficient for

Nicholas to let in a 5ft. tall, dark and well-built person who moved in quickly, very agile for his size. The man was a brigadier in the ISI, the dreaded Intelligence organization of Pakistan and his name was Sher Khan. He handed Nicholas a suitcase stashed with dollars. Nicholas opened the suitcase and flicked through some bundles of notes.

It was the middle of October in 2006, precisely the 15th, and Nicholas's ship was scheduled to leave Dar es Salaam Port of Tanzania within a day or two. The ship would offload tobacco, tea, sugar and linen at different ports. The Aegean Glory was a deep blue cargo ship of 152 meters long and 30 meters breadth, weighing 490 tons.

"How much?" Nicholas asked.

"Ten thousand," Sher Khan answered, "You can count them."

"Where the boxes will be loaded?"

"At the mouth of the river Karnaphuli off the port of Cox Bazaar, Bangladesh."

"Where do you want to offload the boxes?"

"Kidderpore Port."

After the meeting with Nicholas, Sher Khan reached the southern railway station of Brussels and boarded a train that took him to France. In one and a half hours he reached Charles de Gaulle Airport and booked a business class seat in a flight of Air France for Bangkok. At quarter to eight the flight took off towards Bangkok. Looking out of the window he glanced at the illuminated airport. Paris was his favourite city in the world. He relaxed and sipped at champagne.

Two days later, a local operative of the ISI, some key persons from Thailand and Myanmar's underworlds were waiting for Sher Khan in a five-star hotel. They were instrumental in sending arms and ammunition to various insurgent groups in India through sea and land routes. The meeting was delayed as Sher Khan's flight took off an hour late from Paris.

"Sorry, guys," Sher Khan said apologetically after entering the room. He explained his mission to them after which there was a discussion on the implementation aspects. The smugglers of Thailand assured him that they would clear the arms and ammunition from the port of Ranong; they had some trusted excise and customs officers who were on their regular payrolls. The smugglers of Myanmar said they would take the responsibility of delivering those arms and ammunition to the ship, The Aegean Glory, at the mouth of the Karnaphuli River in Bangladesh. After the deal was complete Sher Khan flew back to Karachi, being happy with the way everything was shaping up.

At the port of Karachi a cargo ship was being loaded with products like cotton, yarn, woven fabrics and various articles of leather. At that time a car arrived there and two men got down from the car. They carried five brown boxes to the ship. Captain Abid Hussain was anxiously waiting for them on the deck. He led them to the hold of the ship where they placed those boxes. The ship left Karachi Port on the 25th of October. After five days it entered the port of Ranong in Thailand. Three men were waiting there in a black van, well hidden in darkness. Captain Abid Hussain got off the ship and went to the sandbank. He was wearing sunglasses, even in darkness. He was tall, almost 6'8". Some sailors were standing on the deck. Those boxes were piled beside them. Abid signalled to them to offload the boxes while those three men were ready to take those boxes. The sailors sent those boxes down one by one and those three men stacked them carefully inside the van. When all the boxes were stacked in the van, Abid ordered those three men to start the engine. The van was racing towards Victoria Point, the southernmost tip of the neighbouring country, Myanmar.

Right across the La-un River which is opposite Ranong, there is a small port town of the Union of Myanmar(Burma) whose name is Victoria Point(the name was given by the British), or in Thai it is known as 'Koh Son', or in Burmese, known as 'Kaw Thaung'.

The three men reached Sapaan la, a fish market, in the morning. Opposite the fish market was Victoria Point, the southern tip of Myanmar. The tourists could easily reach Victoria Point, with or without a visa. Long tailed boats would ferry them to and fro continuously. The immigration at the Victoria Point was not strict.

The brown boxes were carefully opened. Inside those boxes, arms and ammunition were lying so innocently. Those arms and ammunition were arrayed in baskets and on them those men spread fish. Then the baskets were taken on a long-tailed boat and ferried to Victoria Point. The immigration officer did not bother to look at the baskets.

A hooded jeep was waiting for them beyond the immigration office. After clearing immigration they started towards Thahtay kyun, a place near the west coast of the Andaman Sea; but they did not go to the beach because they had been given strict orders to transfer those baskets to another black van that would wait on the outskirts of the town.

This time a burly-looking man named Gimy took charge of the baskets. One of the three men stepped forward and asked him, "Hey, are you sure you can take them safely?" But his smile vanished when the cold steel blade of a stiletto touched his chest. His aides wanted to step forward, but looking at Gimy's deadly eyes they retraced.

Gimy drove the van towards a jetty on the beach of the sea. He had specific orders to hand over the van to another man waiting on the beach.

Three days later, after checking out from the security control at Islamabad Airport, a man appeared at the arrival lounge of the airport. His nickname was Moulavi. Children would have been frightened if they could have caught sight of his scary oblong face that had a deep cut mark stretched from the corner of the left eye up to the upper lip. He had a long and crooked nose and quiet surprisingly, his hands were so long that they could touch the knees. His eyes were baleful and his face was covered with a beard in an attempt to hide the cut mark on his face. He was wearing blue denim jeans and a white shirt. In Dubai he was instructed by an ISI agent that a man would wait for him in a corner of the arrival lounge of the airport. That man would be reading the previous day's edition of The Dawn. He had to ask the man, "How was the match?" and he would get the answer, "It'll be held tomorrow." After that he would follow the man who would take him to his destination.

The relatives and office representatives who gathered at the arrival lounge were holding placards to draw the attention of their respective visitors. Moulavi looked around carefully. At one corner he spotted a man, sitting in a chair and reading a copy of The Dawn. He sat beside the man and glanced very cautiously at that newspaper to become sure that it was yesterday's edition, and when he was confirmed it was that very person he was looking for, he asked the same question that he was instructed to utter. The man replied grimly, "It'll be held tomorrow." Then the man stood up and beckoned Moulavi to follow him.

Outside the airport, a sedan was parked with black-tinted windows. The mysterious person opened the front door to let Moulavi in. Within minutes the car started racing down a posh locality in Islamabad- they were heading towards the headquarters of the ISI.

Brigadier Sher Khan was a stocky one-eyed

man. During the India-Pakistan War in the early 1970s he fought in what was then East Pakistan, and lost one eye. After Pakistan lost the war and Bangladesh was formed, he shifted to Islamabad. He was given an option to join the ISI that he accepted gladly because he had immense hatred for the Indians. He was the mastermind behind the latest game plan of the ISI to create a low intensity conflict in India so that the Indian government would remain perennially disturbed and could not concentrate on the more important task surrounding Jammu & Kashmir.

He was waiting for Moulavi, who was his henchman in this operation. When Moulavi arrived at his office, he unfolded the detailed plan before Moulavi.

A huge amount of RDX was already on the way, crossing the Rajasthan border. A cargo ship would go from the port of Cox Bazaar to the port of Kidderpore that would contain a huge consignment of arms and ammunition.

"You've to blow up these pets. The greater number of bodies I can count, the more you get," Sher Khan told Moulavi, whose eyes were glistening in greed.

That night Moulavi flew back to Dubai and then from Dubai he flew to New Delhi. At Indira Gandhi International Airport he showed the security personnel his Dubai visa, quite obviously suppressing his trip to Islamabad.

29th October, Rajasthan. Nasir Ahmed, a truck

driver from Jaipur ferried some boxes full of RDX through a desert trail. He stashed those boxes under the belly of his camel and cloaked them with quilts. Miles after miles of sand stretched across the India Pakistan border. The climate was so inhospitable that people couldn't live there. The density of population was very low. He walked his camel down the hot desert trail strewn with sand dunes. At dusk he reached his house. He stashed the boxes in his house till he got a call on his mobile phone. Next day the much awaited call came. The caller was his cousin brother who was ironically an agent of the ISI. When Nasir went to Karachi, that guy gave him a photo of a person and an address of a house in Old Delhi and told Nasir to memorize them; after that he destroyed the photo and the address in front of Nasir. Nasir was very happy receiving fat packet of money and asked, "When shall I get the next order, brother?"

"First carry out this order and don't be inquisitive; otherwise you'll land yourself into trouble," replied Nasir's brother angrily.

Looking at his petulant face, Nasir didn't dare linger on the conversation.

The same day, after receiving the call, Nasir started his journey to Delhi in his Maruti Van. Some constables were sitting idly at the Gurgaon checkpoint. A sub-inspector was reclining on a motorcycle with his cap pulled halfway on his face. The drivers were handing over money to a constable at the checkpoint. Nasir kept five hundred rupees in the open palm of the constable. Thereafter, he found no policeman who .

stopped his van.

Driving down the dingy lanes of Old Delhi, Nasir stopped his van in front of a deserted house in the evening. The house was in a dilapidated condition. Nasir knocked at the door. A lanky man came out. His face was covered with a beard. It was Moulavi, though Nasir could never know his name because in this dirty game everyone could know only what he was briefed. Moulavi told Nasir to take the boxes inside the house. The lane was deserted at that time; so none saw those boxes.

After the task was completed Nasir drove back and Moulavi sent an e-mail to a recipient at Dubai - "mamaji (uncle) has safely arrived at home."

At night Moulavi flew to Kolkata to meet Salem Ali, a notorious criminal, to brief him on the operation and the ship that was heading towards the port of Kidderpore.

Sanjay Basu, the attaché of the Indian High Commissioner in Islamabad received a phone call at three am on 30th of October. "Hellooo," he yawned drowsily, but was wide awake in the next few seconds. The caller gave him some very important information. Five boxes of arms and ammunition were despatched to Thailand very secretly from the port of Karachi.

Sanjay was actually an undercover agent from RAW, part of India's intelligence network. He encoded the piece of information in an innocent mail: "Uncle is going by sea; receive him." He emailed it to an address in London. The London agent sent it quickly to the headquarters of RAW.

RAW chief Rajat Kapoor was a gaunt-looking person. The high cheek bones and hooked nose gave a dangerous look to his face. He was very tall and sturdy and would bend while walking. Right now he was very nonplussed receiving the mail. A deep furrow was created between his eyebrows while he was smoking his pipe. The room was filled with the sweet smell of Havana tobacco. He wanted to guess the final destination of the arms consignment.

Earlier, he was the chief of the army intelligence. He was well aware of the possible routes through which terrorists and arms were smuggled into India. A large map of India was hanging on the wall. His look was fixed at the north-east border of India.

The Naga insurgency, considered to be the oldest of all insurgent groups operating from the north-east of India, first came to know about the lucrative market of illegal arms ranging from AK47s and RPGs, to numerous types of revolvers and hand grenades that flourished in the illegal markets of Thailand and Myanmar since 80s. The National Socialist Council of Nagaland, better known as the NSCN-IM crossed the Indian border to procure arms from those markets to perpetrate massacre and destruction and later they pulled in other terrorists' organizations like the United Liberation Front of Assam, shortly the ULFA and sold arms to them.

Against this background, the Indian naval intelligence is repeatedly saying that the waters of the Andaman Sea have long been illegally used to send arms to India. Arms would reach the port of Cox bazaar; and then through the extremely dense forest located at the India- Bangladesh border those arms would enter Indian soil.

The impregnable forest with its rugged hilly terrains makes the task of the jawans of the Security Forces, to check such illegal arms import, very difficult. The end result is the earth of North- East India becomes wet with the blood of the jawans and the innocent civilians.

Few years ago a newspaper report created a great stir in the security circle when the Bangladeshi Joint Forces, being tipped by some informer, could seize 10 truckloads of submachine guns, AK47s, submachine carbines, Chinese pistols, rocket shells, launchers, hand grenades and huge amount of bullets from 1500 wooden boxes from the port area of Cox Bazaar.

"Maybe the Naga insurgent groups have procured those arms," thought Rajat.

He telephoned the chief of the army intelligence and passed on the information and gave his analysis about the possible destination of the consignment. Consequently, the army at the Myanmar-India border was put on high alert. Meanwhile, Rajat secretly visited some special persons. They were the leaders of the Kachen Liberation Army, a group who were fighting for the freedom of Arakan from Myanmar. Those leaders were hiding in a remote village of Mizoram to avoid arrest by the police of Myanmar.

The meeting was arranged by the DGP of the Border Security Force. The whole business was kept so clandestine that only the Prime Minister and the Chief Minister knew about the meeting, while all other ministers or officers were kept in darkness about his visit.

The leaders were kept in a hut and their safety and security was the onus of the Border Security Force. Rajat asked them, "Do you know what the hell the ship from Pakistan was doing at the port of Ranong?"

But they had no information.

"We're not involved in this consignment. Maybe the LTTE have procured the arms," they suggested.

"Bull shit!" snorted Rajat, "our friends are more interested in sending arms to the Indian insurgents." He told them to find out who had ordered the consignment.

After three days they brought him a piece of news that completely misled him. They informed him that the consignment was ordered by some smugglers of Thailand who would sell the arms to the LTTE.

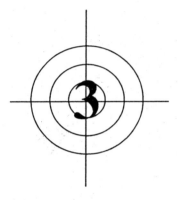

The dark salty water of the Andaman Sea was lapping a wooden jetty. Some labourers were carrying the baskets, which came from the port of Ranong, to a speedboat that was tethered to the jetty. A burly-looking man whose name was Robert Grut was overseeing their work. His steely eyes made it clear that he could kill anyone without any remorse - a perfect butcher indeed! A rifle was slung from his shoulder.

The jetty was not used for a long time because of its derelict condition and hence no boat came there. The place was deserted; save a tree whose long branches were overhanging the waters and some front leaves touched the stream, sometimes creating a rustling sound.

The sky was overcast with black puffy clouds and no wind was blowing. Two men were sitting on the boat smoking cigarettes. "It might rain," one of them commented. The other man who was older did not reply; he only cast a surly look at the sky and spat on the sea.

The black van that carried those five baskets was stationed nearby. The labourers were offloading the baskets from it, before carrying them to the boat. That those baskets were heavy was evident from the strenuous look on their faces.

After the baskets were loaded on the boat, Robert came to the jetty and signalled to the boatmen to start the boat. Then he returned to the black van. Within seconds the driver started the engine. The boat was heading towards Bangladesh, or to be more specific, its destination was the port of Cox Bazaar. The baskets were stacked under the flat wooden floor of the boat and covered with fishing nets. On the floor were stacked some big buckets to make it look like a fishing boat of Myanmar.

Myanmar has a long coastline of nearly 2,000 km. It can be divided into three coastal regions: the Rakhine Coastal Region from the mouth of the Naaf River to Mawtin Point, about 740 km in length, the Irrawaddy Delta and the Gulf of Moattama (Martaban) Coastal Region from the Mawtin Point to the Gulf of Moattama, about 460 km in length, and the Thanintharyi Coastal Region extending from the Gulf of Moattama to the mouth of the Pakchan River, about 800 km in length in the Bay of Bengal and in the Andaman Sea.

At night a heavy rain started with a strong gale but those boatmen were ready for it. They quickly brought out a large plastic sheet and spread it on the baskets. Next day they crossed the Andaman Sea and entered the Bay of Bengal. So far they had not encountered any navy vessel either from India or Bangladesh, but now a navy ship of Myanmar cropped up. The captain asked them where they were going. The elderly man said in Burmese that they belonged to Thahtay kyun and they were looking for shrimps, which was natural as many Burmese boats would venture into the sea for shrimps. The captain let them go but also warned them not to enter into Bangladesh territory. With a grin the boatmen nodded their heads; but as soon as the ship left the place they headed towards Chittagong. After two days they reached the mouth of the river Karnaphuli. The port was twelve miles inward from the mouth of the river.

The cargo ship, 'Aegean Glory', was anchored at the mouth of the river. Captain Nicholas Gorskov was standing on the deck watching the sea through binoculars. The setting sun cast a long mournful light on the ship. As soon as the boat appeared on the horizon a sinister smile waved across his mouth. He ordered the sailors to drop the ladders from the ship.

Three sailors climbed down the ladders when

the boat stopped beside the ship. The boatmen removed the planks and showed the baskets. The sailors tied those baskets with strong ropes and signalled to the other sailors who were standing on the deck of the ship, to pull the baskets on the deck. One by one all five baskets were taken on the ship. Thereafter, the boat left the place to return to Myanmar.

Nicholas got strict orders from Sher Khan that the baskets had to be wrapped up in the bales of linen; so that no one could suspect anything.

At midnight he got an order from Sher Khan to start the ship towards the port of Kidderpore.

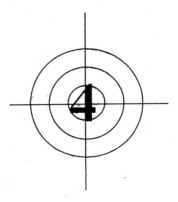

A deluxe room of a five-star hotel in Kolkata was booked online from Dhaka. The booking was made from a merchant office in Dhaka. Two men arrived at the hotel and showed the booking confirmation receipt that the hotel issued online. A cute receptionist welcomed them with a honey-laden smile. Few minutes later they reached their room with a porter. One was an ISI officer Khoda Baksh and the other was Saukat Chowdhury, a hardcore member of the Harkat ul Jihadii Islam from Bangladesh, popularly known as the HuJI-B.

After the porter departed, they thoroughly checked the room and the toilet to be assured that there was no hidden camera or voice recorder. Half an hour later the receptionist called them to inform that some visitors had arrived at the hotel and they wanted to meet Khoda Baksh. They requested the receptionist to send the visitors to the room. After initial greetings, one of the visitors spread a local area map of North Bengal and another explained the locations of the important army installations, government offices, and railway stations to Khoda Baksh.

Khoda Baksh told the visitors, "We're sending some consignment by sea. In due course of time we'll inform you where you've to collect them. But this time headquarters wants a major strike in North Bengal." There was such a menace in his voice that the visitors were alarmed. Jatin Barma, the area commander of the Kamtapur Liberation Organization, who had come specifically for this meeting, meekly said, "Yes, sir. This time we'll blow up some major army installations."

Khoda Baksh looked at him and asked, "Why is the KLO (Kamtapur Liberation Organization) not striking the police in North Bengal? We need results from you."

"Sir, we need weapons and RDX for that. We told Saukat that we need some revolvers and bullets immediately, but till now we have got none."

"What's your local contact doing?" Khoda Baksh asked Saukat angrily.

"Sir, the security is very tough nowadays. But I'll talk to our contacts so that they can send these items in a day or two," Saukat hurriedly replied.

After the departure of the visitors, they left for the airport and flew to Dhaka. Khoda Baksh waited in the airport to board another plane that would take him to Islamabad. Saukat came out from the airport. A car was waiting for him in the parking lot. He was going to the headquarters of the dreadful terrorist organization, the HuJI-B. He was engrossed in deep thought.

Khoda Baksh had passed to him a very important order that he had to carry out. He contacted Salem by mobile phone and ordered him to deliver two revolvers and some bullets to Jatin in a day or two. After that he contacted Jatin and told him that a man would go to the Blue Diamond hotel in Siliguri to deliver the revolvers and bullets. He told Jatin that he would inform him the exact time and date of the delivery in a day or two. When the Aegean Glory would leave for the port of Kidderpore he had to cross the Indo-Bangladesh border. There he would meet the leaders of the terrorists to chalk out a blueprint to blow the targets like army camps, bridges and trains.

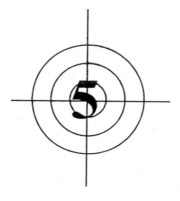

Boris Flusfeder carried a stool to his bedroom and stood on it to place a fresh garland of tuberose on Maya's photograph. Few drops of tears rolled down his cheeks. Then he went to the window and looked out. A martin was crying on the roof of the servant's quarters for a long time. A cold wind started to blow from last night; a signal that winter was knocking at the door. He thought about London. Though he had never visited the City, David Flusfeder, his father, used to tell him so many stories about the City that he felt very much familiar with it. David had a pub at Leicester Square. His first wife, Hannah, was an Irish, who died in a plane crash while going to visit her parents in Chicago. The tragedy beset him and put him in depression for a long time. Then Maya came in his life, through a strange situation.

Maya came to London with her lover, Aneek, who she met in Kolkata when she visited her maternal uncle's home during the summer vacation. She was a high school student at that time. At that time Aneek also came home from London. His parents would live in a house that was adjacent to her maternal uncle's. As she was very beautiful, he was easily attracted to her. He himself was also tall and handsome. They soon began to meet in parks and restaurants. When he was going back to London, he proposed to her and told her, "Maya, I love you and I want to marry you." She believed him. He helped her get a passport and a short visit visa.

He told her that he was an engineer, but when she arrived in London, she discovered that he had duped her. Actually, he was a waiter in an Indian restaurant; still, she could not accuse him of cheating her, because he promised her that he would soon marry her. But the scoundrel made a contract with his boss- the owner of the restaurant- that he would marry his mentally retarded daughter. Maya could not know it till everything was finalised.

David found her at Leicester Square. One day when he was standing outside his pub, one of his staff members noticed her and told him, "Master! A girl is crying." David saw a pretty young woman was sobbing bitterly, sitting on a kerbstone of the pavement. His experienced eyes understood that she had been jilted by someone and now she had nowhere to go. Though she was in a shabby condition he understood that she came from a good family. He told his young Indian waiter to talk to her.

That youth translated Maya's story to David. He took her home and opened the guest room for her. Then he told her that she could live in his house as long as she wished. She nodded her head in gratitude.

After Hannah's death David decided that he would never marry, but he soon fell in love with Maya.

One day she announced, "I want to work in the pub."

"Really!"

He was hesitating, but she was determined. She soon began to attend the pub. She was intelligent. She very quickly adapted herself to the pub culture; she would supervise the waiters, look after the visitors, and she even picked up the typical pub banter. The local people who would frequent the pub were pleasantly surprised when they noticed a young Indian girl deftly speaking their language.

David proposed to her exactly one year later. They were married in a local Protestant Church. After one year she gave birth to a son. They named the boy Boris, who was like his mother, medium height, soft-minded, pale-complexioned; but his eyes were as blue as blue bells, like his father's.

Unfortunately, their happy life could not last long as she died shortly after a bad bout of pneumonia. At her deathbed David promised that he would go to India and raise Boris there.

With little Boris he arrived in Bibeknagar, where Maya's parents would live. He heard from Maya that her father had died long ago, but her mother would live there with her brother. That old woman began to cry when she came to know Boris was her daughter's son. She requested David to live in Bibeknagar. He couldn't dishearten the old woman and began to live there. Later, he set up a school in Bibeknagar in memory of Maya.

When Boris finished his education he took charge of the school. David gave his hand in marriage to an Indian girl named Sonali. In Bibeknagar his only friend was Pramath Biswas.

Boris was like his mother, always eager to help the poor and the distressed. Bibeknagar station was crowded with beggars, urchins, abandoned women and old men. They would live under the terrace of the station, beside the booking counters, on the foot-bridge, and in the platforms. After people would return home, Boris would stroll in the station area. When he would see the plight of those people a nameless pain would assail him; a turbulence of emotion would surge inside him; a great depression would sit on his heart like deadweight; life would seem to him tasteless; and a feel of must-I-do-something would chase him.

Those poor people would cook some rotten vegetables or if luck would have it, some piece of fish or meat, thrown away from the local hotels. The utensils they used were earthen pots whose outer walls were smudged with carbon. Two bricks were used as props to put the pots; and some leaves and dry twigs that they could collect from the roadside trees would serve as fuel. As the fire would leap up the starved faces would become eager.

There were some lunatics who would scavenge food from the heap of garbage piled up beside the food stalls. A brawl would often start between those lunatics and the street dogs that also depended on the trash for food.

When the night would become denser, they would lie either on the bare pavement or on torn pieces of clothes. After that the human predators would come out for their prey. Those human-ogres would drag some helpless women in the dark corners to feed their lust. In due course of time those women would deliver children. During pregnancy their condition would become even worse as they could not do any work to get food.

During one of his frequent night strolls, Boris found a poor child crying bitterly under the tall column that would support the arcade of the station. Both his legs were infected with sores and pus and blood was coming out from the sores. Boris stood beside him and asked softly, "What's your name?"

"Raghu," the boy answered. Boris came to know from him that his drug-addict stepfather would flog him mercilessly if he could not give him money. Then one day he ran away from home and wandered from place to place, shoplifting to meet hunger, sleeping under the footbridges. With Boris's help the boy got a shelter in the orphanage which Pramath would frequent.

Every year in the month of February, Uncle Ned, Aunt Sheila and Cousin Morris would visit Bibeknagar. They would live in Soho, where Uncle Ned had a restaurant. This year they were very eager to come to Bibeknagar and meet Sonali because she was pregnant. Umpteen times they requested Boris to visit London, but each time he could not make it due to some problem or the other. This time Boris promised that Sonali and he would definitely visit London with their newborn baby.

Boris looked at the clock. "Pramath should have reached," he thought. He decided to meet Pramath to discuss certain matters about his school. He went to the study and looked at the letter that had come from the secretary of the school. He heard the chime of the church bell. Some sparrows were chirping on the windowsills of the building. A squirrel climbed a mango tree hoisting its tail.

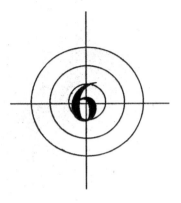

Sitting on a wooden bench beneath a deodar tree, Pramath was waiting for a train. Last night he attended a programme held in an orphanage in Kantinagar, he was attached to. The programme ended late at night and he could not return home. He stayed in his aunt's house. Coincidentally, she had donated the land for the orphanage.

It was an early winter morning. At quarter past six a local train arrived at the platform, loaded with sacks of vegetables that the farmers were bringing from the villages. When the train stopped at the platform, passengers tried to board the train; but those huge sacks were so awkwardly stacked at the entrance of each compartment that some sort of chaos was created among the passengers in front of each compartment. The passengers who were mostly office-goers were abusing the farmers because they could not enter the compartments.

Arching his body, Pramath advanced through the crowd. Luckily, he spotted a seat whose occupant stood up to get down at the next station. Pramath went there to make room for him on the vacant seat. When the train started moving in slow motion, he saw a vendor was walking down the platform with a bunch of newspapers. He called out to the man who folded an English newspaper and passed it to him through the open window. He put a two-rupee coin on the extended palm of the vendor.

At Bibeknagar station Pramath got down from the train and crossing over the footbridge, reached the autorickshaw stand. The clock atop the station building was showing a quarter to seven. The old station road went westward for a couple of yards before dividing into two; one branch turned left; and the other entered the cantonment area.

The houses on either side of the road were wrapped up in dense fog. Some stray dogs were searching for food in a heap of stale eggshells beside a fast-food stall. The street dwellers that slept the night on the pavements were rolling their torn mattress in preparation for another day of drudgery. Some labourers were slowly walking along the footpath. The school buses were whizzing students to the local English-medium schools. An urchin was looking at the large glass door of a departmental store, clutching a torn jute bag, hanging from his fragile shoulder.

When the autorickshaw was entering the cantonment area, Pramath heard the sound of an explosion. Craning his neck outside the vehicle, he saw that a screen of smoke was spiraling heavenward; and on the street a youth was lying in a pool of blood. The mutilated body was wriggling in pain. Panic stricken, the driver accelerated the speed of the vehicle. As a result, the cool November wind swept across Pramath's face.

A large hoarding supported by two strong iron poles welcomed him. On its left side a plaque was placed on a stone podium rounded by a stout iron chain. A brief history of the cantonment was inscribed on that stone plaque.

Since the East India Company found Bibeknagar very suitable for the movement of their troops, they built a large cantonment for the accommodation of two batteries of artillery, the wing of a regiment and two battalions of soldiers. And besides, there were the Governor's house, a cathedral, a wharf, a racecourse and a menagerie.

As in England Gothic became the preferred style of architecture during Queen Victoria's regime, the effect was equally found on the old constructions inside the cantonment. The distinctive features of Gothic style, like the pointed arch, vault, crocket, aisle, tall large clustered columns, heavy ornamental design, the carvings, the magnanimous structure that easily created a majestic feel in the mind of the viewers, were closely followed while building the cathedral, the Governor's house and even the station building. The British would fondly call the place their "little England". Governor- General Lord Dalhousie commented in his writing, "It is charming and reconciles me to a residence in Bengal more than anything else has yet done ...a pretty pleasure ground, a beautiful garden, an aviary, a menagerie, and all situated on the bank of the river and surrounded by a park quite home like in its palms and mangoes, for oaks and elms, larch and beech." When he would visit the place the message would go out from Fort William to Bibeknagar, often with a boom of cannon along the bank of the Ganga.

Lady Charlotte Canning also found the place very charming, as she wrote, "The luxuriant growth in the jungle ground outside of dazzling greens during the rains is more beautiful than I can describe and I always think of the Palm House at Kew which gives a fair idea of it."

Pramath noticed that St. Bartholomew Cathedral was standing in quiet foggy silence. At the riverside bus stop Pramath left the autorickshaw and began walking. On the left side of the road some men were sitting on the bank of a large tank. They were looking at the end of their fishing rods with the concentration of Arjuna of the Mahabharata, the famous hero of the great Indian epic. The riverside road wound its way for a quarter of a mile before stopping in front of a wharf on the Ganga. The wharf was known as "Queen's Ghat". The Cantonment Board's jurisdiction ended at the left side of the wharf and the jurisdiction of the local municipality stretched from the right side of the wharf up to the local court.

The cantonment was flanked on both sides by two municipalities. Towards the east stood two state government offices - the police station and an old, dilapidated labour office, each looking over and grimacing at the other. The station was a big, red-coloured building with the top of a medieval castle. The station compound was littered with innumerable fast-food stalls and encroached with autorickshaws, creating a claustrophobic feel for the people.

There were two popular cinemas - the Eden Hall, and the Ahindra Hall. For many years thousands of viewers would throng there. Sometimes the police had to intervene to control the rush of the viewers. When the cable television entered people's bedrooms, those two halls began to fade in darkness due to utter neglect. None would care to look at them, even in reminiscence; save a handful of old timers.

Pramath's house was on the right side of the wharf. It was a big, square bungalow that had been dazzling white and majestically adorned with stylish domes and scrolled staircase. Recently, the owner of an auto garage and a tea-stall occupied some portion of the boundary wall and part of the decorative front gate, and hung strips of tobacco packets from the gate. Some youths would also perch on the front wall. They would talk among themselves shouting slang, chewing tobacco and betel leaves, and would spray red betel-juice from their mouth aiming at the wall. As a result the wall was coated with patches of red saliva.

The house stood on a large ground quite cozily surrounded by a lofty wall. The front part was landscaped with posh green turf and various flower plants. A gravel path led the way through the green to the portico. A 1950 Austin was parked there permanently. The front door opened to a big drawing room where some furniture - one sofa settee, two chairs, and a teak wood table- was arranged in the middle. Those were made in Victorian style - heavy proportions, dark, polished, highly ornamental and cushioned with high density coir. Two large Italian book cases were resting against the walls.

Gourav, Pramath"s father, was a connoisseur of art. He culled two oil paintings in large rosewood frames, one showing a London mail coach passing a fox hunt in the background and the other showing two coaches running in competition. Beside the staircase, there stood a replica of Auguste Rodin's 'The Thinker'. On the right side of the room were the dining room and the kitchen. The staircase spiraled to the first floor. The first floor had four rooms, each with attached bathroom. The floor of each room was covered with rich persian carpet. The door and the windows were shaped like flamboyant arches with tracery on surface, and stained glass on the leaded windows.

The southern room was allotted to Pramath and his wife, Pratima. A four poster bed made of mahogany wood stood at the centre of the bedroom. Opposite it was standing a wardrobe whose legs were designed with flowers, leaves, and angels. Beside the headboard of the bed was kept a lamp on a nightstand. The corners of the room were adorned with designed shelves; but the most beautiful was a Venetian mirror whose ornate design would earn praise from the visitors. Gourav was a renowned lawyer of Calcutta High Court. Since Pramath was his only son, he hoped that Pramath would step into his profession; but Pramath wanted to be an army officer.

Like his father, he was very tall, hawk-nosed; he had the same eagle eyes, the same haughty cheekbones covered with wheat-colored skin, and the same ox like broad shoulders. He joined the Indian Army as a commissioned captain in the 2nd Rajputana Rifles.

The Rajputana Rifles is the senior most regiment of the Indian Army. The jawans of this regiment played crucial role for establishing the British Empire which can easily be understood from the historical background, when the British were trying to defeat the rising Marathas in one hand and the rival French on the other hand for establishing undisputed supremacy over India. These jawans who are otherwise very simple persons of certain areas of Maharastra and Gujrat are dangerous soldiers on the battlefields. From Italy to Abyssinia, France to China, they brought victories for the British Empire, each time enduring immense physical pain under extreme conditions on the battlefields. They never fear to face the enemies' bullets and hand-to-hand fights; and despite receiving severe injuries they never retreat from the battlefields.

Immediately after Independence of India, when Pakistan sent the tribal forces to Kashmir to capture the state, the Indian government sent forces. At that time beside other regiments the jawans of the Rajputana Rifles fought valiantly at the mountains of Kashmir and routed the enemies.

Hence when the Kargil War broke out, they were brought back into action.

Pramath had some great experiences during the Kargil War. On the 8th of May in 1999 he was sitting in his office when the message came from New Delhi that the Pakistani Army had occupied tops of Tiger Hill. He was given the order to clear the heights of Tiger Hill. He and his jawans had to fight the Pakistani forces in the treacherous terrains. During their uphill march to recapture point 5100 they lost two of their efficient officers and ten jawans. The route advanced through a green valley stretched from the east to the west. To the east were small villages nestled on the slopes leading up to Tiger Hill but enemy's shells battered those villages. The roofs, door frames, window frames were shattered, and brick walls crumbled down. The people fled from their villages many days ago, and an eerie silence reigned there; but nature forgot the enemy's presence, and bedecked the entire area with a plethora of roses and wagtails and other flowers. At a glance nothing seemed wrong, but the enemy's shells soon fell on the ground creating great craters.

Pramath found more jawans were killed, their dead bodies were sent to the base camp wrapped in bags, but there was no sign of panic among the jawans. They were moving upward till they reached the trench of the enemies. That was the darkest side of the war. They advanced the enemy's trench at night and jumped inside the trench. Then was started the most primitive brutal war. Charging of bayonet and human cries rent the sky making the atmosphere heavy. When the day broke, the trench was a heap of dead bodies.

The river that was leaping down through the

deep gorges with a ferocity that any human who dared go to it would have been swept away by its current was now slow and heavy with corpses. The guns that were surreptitiously located in the caves of the hill, so far howling their flame and fury, were now silent.

After routing the enemies from Tiger Hill, when Pramath and his jawans were waiting for the next order, the news reader of All India Radio suddenly announced that the enemies had been defeated and they had fled from the tops of the hills. Pramath and his jawans hugged one another amidst joy and relief.

During the operation an enemy's bullet hit him on his left shoulder. After the war was over, he accepted voluntary retirement and engaged himself in another pursuit of life - that was serving the orphans.

There was a funny incident about his marriage. He feared that the girl who would be his wife could not like his profession; hence he decided not to marry. One day his parents told him that they had arranged his marriage and he had to go with them to visit the girl.

They reached the girl's house in the afternoon. Pramath noticed that an extraordinarily beautiful woman was coming towards him. Her eyes were as deep as the sea; complexion, as white as snow; nose, as thin as a flute; and the lips, as red as pomegranate. Pramath felt that his senses were getting numb before such ravishing beauty. At one point he began to think that this beauty would be his wife; but again he recalled his mission in life.

That night he wrote a letter to that girl: "I've

fallen in your love, Pratima, but I'm scared that your love may distract me from my duty to my country. I'm confused. I can't miss you, but at the same time I can't bury my idealism. Throughout the night I've tried to balance between you and my idealism. Now, I realize that I'm wrong. I've to take a decision. I've cherished some dream that I must fulfill. I've to show the grit to pursue my dream. I've to take a decision independently though I'm afraid you may be hurt. Now, when life has been gracious enough to show me the truth, I want to devote myself to the service of my country. Please excuse me, Pratima. I can't marry you because I've realized that I can't be a successful family man. I can't make you happy. If my father insists that I marry you, then I will leave home so that I can save my dream."

He met Boris with the letter and requested him to deliver it to Pratima. Boris opposed vehemently; but Pramath made him do the job.

The result was not pleasant for Pramath. That particular letter duly reached his father; he was called up to his father's chamber and got a sound scolding from Gourav.

Three months later Pramath and Pratima tied the nuptial bond.

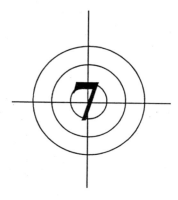

When Pramath returned home, he saw that his wife was not at home. Mumpi, his elder daughter, was waiting for him. He asked her, "Won't you go to your computer centre today?"

"I was waiting for you. Take your food in time and also tell mom not to worry about me. I'll be late."

"Where has your mom gone?"

"Our uncle's home. By the way, don't forget to take your medicine in time," she threw in the order while rushing towards the door.

Pramath looked at her receding figure with an affectionate smile. He was very fond of his daughter. She was tall. Her eyes were very deep like her mother's.

Sonai, his son, was born after five years of their marriage. Mumpi was born after one year of their marriage. Pramath was twenty-five when he married and now he was fifty. When Sonai was born, Pramath was posted in Kashmir. He could not come home. Pratima raised the child alone; hence the boy was more attached to Pratima.

Nowadays Pramath's health was not going well. Two days ago he visited a doctor. He expected that Sonai would accompany him, but he refused to go. He told Pramath that he had some important classes in college. Pramath felt sorry, but did not express it. When he was going out Mumpi told him, "I'm coming with you."

"Won't you go to computer centre?" he was surprised.

She said that she had taken leave from office so that she could go with him.

Mumpi worked in a local computer centre. After Mumpi left, Pramath refreshed himself and went to the garden. A week ago he had purchased some saplings of petunia and stacked them at one corner of the garden. Today he decided to plant them. He selected a place at one corner of the garden, removed the weeds with a scythe and then planted those saplings.

After lunch he took a novel and reclined on the bed. He had an old habit of reading a book before taking a nap. When he woke up, it was half past five. Hastily, he put on a wrapper and after locking the front door, came out on the street.

The tall teak trees that grew on either side of the road looked somber at the advent of winter. The old banyan trees, young mango trees, large gulmohar trees were peeping over the compound wall of the army officers' bungalows. Pramath would always feel that the place had a typical feel of Victorian aristocracy. Some organizations had also set up buildings with the permission of the Board.

The path stretched few yards and then stopped outside a park which was a popular haunt for the lovers. To beautify the park, the Board engaged a private agency who created half a dozen groves where the lovers could spend honeyed moments in the charming embraces of each other. Pramath did not enter the park; rather he turned right, and stopped in front of Boris's house.

Boris was very excited.

"Do you know what happened in the morning? A youth was slain in our neighborhood. People are saying that Salem has killed the youth; but you see the police will not arrest him because he is very powerful. There is a rumour in the air that Salem has become a jihadi and supplies the terrorists with arms," Boris said.

"I don't believe all these nonsense. Unlike other states, religious ambience of our state is pretty good. Here the politicians are not corrupt and the religious atmosphere is also secular," Pramath asserted.

"You have no idea about Salem," Boris scoffed

at him for his ignorance.

"Then, why don't the police arrest him?" Pramath argued.

Pramath did not notice that the clock had struck eight. When Boris drew his attention to the clock, he jumped to his feet. After reaching home, he saw that Pratima was pacing in the lawn and her face was knotted with anger.

Seeing him she blew her top. "Have you lost your senses? You know very well that I would return in the evening. Then why did you go out?" she shouted.

He tried to explain the cause of his delay but his words were drowned helplessly amidst the torrent of her words.

He unlocked the door. On the dining table she noticed some unwashed plates and dishes. "Certainly, the maidservant could not enter the house. When did you go out?" she asked him indignantly.

"I left home at 5.30, but before that I was at home because I know that she comes between four and five." He tried to explain.

"Then you were sleeping and couldn't hear the doorbell," She declared her opinion in a conclusive manner. Pramath did not dare argue with her.

"I'm cleaning the plates," he told her coaxingly.

"No thanks. I can do it myself." She at once dismissed him. After changing her dress, she went into the kitchen. Half an hour later she appeared in the drawing room with two teas.

Meanwhile, Pramath was watching the news on television. Seeing Pratima in front of him, he asked, "How are your brothers?"

"They were enquiring about your health," she replied sharply.

"I'll talk to them. Oh, I forgot to tell you that Mumpi had informed me she'd be late."

"This girl is increasing my BP day by day," she said excitedly.

"Don't worry. She will be all right." He tried to placate her.

"Can't you see anything? Her intimacy with Afroj is growing. A mishap will soon befall her. By the way, I asked you to talk to the pundit. What about it?"

"I've told him." He faltered because he had promised to talk to the pundit, but forgot all about it after he went to the orphanage.

"I'll see what you do when some mishap takes place," she said very angrily.

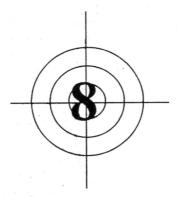

After her duty was over in the computer centre, Mumpi was waiting for Afroj Roy in front of a local auditorium. Half an hour ago he had contacted her from office to inform that he was boarding a train. A local club arranged a programme of a popular band of Kolkata in the auditorium. As she was an ardent fan of that band, she purchased two tickets. When he arrived at the auditorium, the programme had already started. Grabbing his hand she hurtled towards the hall. Inside the hall, the show was in full swing. The band was singing the hit numbers and the audience was clapping and whistling to encourage them.

She told him excitedly, "Look, they are playing my favourite numbers!" At the end of the programme she went backstage to get the autographs of the singers.

The programme ended at half past eleven. The last bus had already left at eleven. They started walking. Few others were also walking; but at the crossing they took a different route. Only Afroj and Mumpi were walking down the road that was desolate beyond the Army Base Hospital. They were walking together, very close to each other. He kept his right arm around her waist, and let his head lean against hers. She was crooning the lyric of one of her favourite numbers that she had listened only minutes before. At Queen's Ghat bus stop the street lamp was out of order. Some youths in the 18-20 age-groups were squatting beneath a tree and smoking ganja. Initially, Mumpi and Afroj couldn't notice them, as the tree was hidden under a sheet of darkness; but when they were crossing it, one guy from the gang darted slang words at Mumpi, "What a sexy piece, man!"

She pretended that she had not heard the comment; but Afroj couldn't put up with that offence. He stepped towards them and asked sternly, "Which of you said it?"

He focused his torch on them. At that time her attention fell on the boy, sitting at the corner of the tree, and saw to her utter surprise that her own younger brother Sonai was present there.

When Sonai saw that he had been identified, he jumped up instantly and covering his face with both hands, ran towards the Queen's Ghat.

"Why are you talking to some goons?" she told off Afroj.

"These rascals should not be spared at all," protested Afroj; but she was not listening to him, because she was highly perplexed by such an unexpected discovery.

"Why did you hold me back? I could teach them a good lesson," he told her grudgingly.

"Will you stop, please?" she cried out suddenly.

He was surprised, finding no apparent reason for her anger; but at the same time he kept silent during the rest of the walk. At the entrance of the house, she parted from him after a very curt and dry kiss.

Once home she asked Pratima, "Where is Sonai?" Seeing her anxious face Pratima understood that some untoward incident had occurred. "How can I know where he is?" she flung the question.

Mumpi came home with a faint hope at the bottom of her heart that perhaps she might be wrong, perhaps he was not there among those scum; but when she heard that he was not at home, her hopes frittered away. She told her mother, "Send him to my room whenever he returns. I've some important business with him."

Sonai returned home past midnight. Pratima was waiting for him. She asked him with a mild reproach, "Is it the time to return home? Your elder sister is waiting for you in her room. Visit her at once."

Mumpi decided to ask her brother what he was doing there with those rascals. Hearing his voice in the dining room, she came out from her bedroom and ordered him to meet her at once. When he appeared in her room, she greeted him with a sardonic smile and told him scornfully, "What the hell were you doing with those scum?"

"I'm very sorry, sis. They didn't know that you are my sister," he answered lightly.

"Impossible! I'm born and bred here. I know very well that they are simply antisocial elements," she cried out, "I must talk to dad."

"Do whatever you wish," Sonai said, highly frustrated; and then he left the room, slamming the door behind him.

After he left the room, Mumpi bolted the door. A full deep cry was gushing forth from her inside which was beyond her control to suppress. She thought that her brother, who saved up Rs. 1,000 from his pocket money to buy gifts for her birthday, was now cozying up to some ruffians.

But how could she tell it to her parents! They would be so upset.

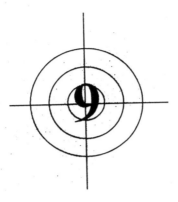

Sonai went to the roof after the quarrel with Mumpi. "Certainly, dad will drive me out of home if Mumpi discloses the truth." He shivered, just imagining the reaction of his father.

He was a student of Scottish Church College in Kolkata. Dev and Kumar were his bosom friends in the college. Dev Chatterjee came from a family that had a traditional printing business. He would live in an old-fashioned two-storied house in Shyambazar. Kumar's father, Mihir Paul, was a realtor. Once Kumar told them that his father was a union leader of a jute mill. Later, he started the realty business when the boom in this sector began. His critics would say that some political leaders and criminals were also associated with him.

Three friends would often play truant from the college and spend hours together at videogame-parlours. Sometimes they would wander around the shopping malls and the multiplexes, not so much for shopping or viewing movies, but for ogling the girls.

Dev was their leader. Once he said, "There is no point in pursuing studies. It's just a waste of time. Look at our dads. None of them has studied in college; but how smoothly they are making big bucks!"

At that time Sonai said, "My maternal uncles also run a big pharmaceutical company."

"Then why are you sticking here?" they wondered.

"Dad says that I've to study hard if I want to shine in life."

"Your dad is a crazy man. In today's world none slips up such a golden opportunity."

Though there were plenty of girls in the college, Sonai had no girl friend with whom he went on a date. Three months ago, on a summer night he was returning from Dev's house. It was pretty late, around ten o'clock; some passengers were sitting inside the train compartment ; a young girl was sitting in front of him. There are always some girls who can draw your attention. He was looking at her stealthily, hesitating to start a conversation.

After few minutes the girl herself asked him, "Going far?"

"Bibeknagar," Sonai replied.

"Where do you live?" she asked again. He told her his address.

"I'm Puma. I live at 49 Robertson Road. I'm returning from Salt Lake. I'm doing a fashion designing course there." She held the thread of the conversation.

"I have noticed the house. It is just opposite the auditorium. It is already late. May I escort you to your house?"

She accepted his offer.

Before leaving her at the doorstep, he asked her, "Can we meet tomorrow?"

"I'll wait for you near the booking counter at nine p.m."

Next day he was waiting for her near the booking counter. He was wearing a navy blue jacket that his elder maternal uncle had once brought for him from New York. He was looking quiet smart and confident. At half past nine she appeared there. He looked at her in appreciation, because she was wearing a short top and a pair of skin-hugging jeans. He proposed, "Let's go to the Blue Dragon."

They chose a table in a corner. Light music was playing on a jukebox. A cool calm environment was prevailing in the room. A waiter smartly strolled towards them with a menu card. She ordered prawn salad and honey noodles for both of them. They were talking over dinner.

"We have a pharmaceutical company," Sonai said

deliberately to impress her.

"You are an industrialist!" She looked at him with keen interest.

Before going back home they decided they would meet regularly. At night he told Pratima, "I need some five thousand bucks." She was watching some TV serials in the drawing room.

"Why do you need this amount?" she wanted to know.

"I need the bucks to buy some books." He lied to her.

"Your dad gave you pocket money, didn't he?" she asked.

"You won't understand. Give me the money," he said impatiently.

Next day when they met they decided they should visit South City mall. "It's so gorgeous. I frequent the place." Her eyes were shining in a crazy tremor. There she made him purchase a small purse for her that cost him four thousand rupees. "You're so sweet," she twitched his cheeks.

After attending classes, he would go to her college. In fact, it became his daily routine. Then they would go to different places. It was Puma, who would select where they should go; their destination was various shopping malls. Whenever she would step inside a mall he would become tensed, as he had to pay and he got only two thousand rupees as pocket money from his father.

Puma's father was the director of a Jute Research Institute and her mother was a doctor in a government hospital. Both had busy schedules, so Puma was brought up under the tutelage of an Anglo Indian governess. From childhood she loved to lead a flamboyant social life with friends; she was also very daring in her attitude and dressing style; and she would often go in tight tops and miniskirts to the college. One day she was called up to the principal's office. She sat on the table in front of him showing a clear cleavage. "You can come to college in whatever dress you like. Please, don't come here again," the principal told her.

When their relation became a month old, Puma invited Sonai to her home to introduce him to her parents. Then she took him to her room; and there she flung her arms around his shoulder and told him, "Kiss me."

He was not prepared for such offer; he felt his knees were knocking fast and heart was racing as if it was running at the final lap in the Derby. She said impatiently, "Come on." He tried to advance, but stumbled on her feet.

"Fool!" she sniffed at his clumsy attempt.

Sonai could not suspect that some local thugs were keeping a watch on his relationship with Puma. One day while he was returning home at night, they besieged him at Queen's Ghat bus stop and forcibly led him to their club. Their leader, Afjal, told him, "Rascal! You are screwing that beautiful girl." They then poured some country liquor into his throat and ordered him to dance to a filmy tune. After that they would force him to visit the club regularly.

After the altercation with Mumpi, he went to the club the next morning. There was an old building at the entrance of the road where the club was situated. The ground floor was a marketplace and it was buzzing with the conversation between the buyers and the sellers. In the dim yellow light hanging from the ceiling, the fish-sellers were cutting prawns, sardines, shrimps, and carps with skilled hand. At one corner there was a long queue in front of a meat shop. The butcher was busy cutting goats. Those who were standing in the queue were shouting, "You're cheating us. Give us meat, not bones!" The sly butcher was giving meat to the veteran buyers; but to those who were new he was passing some bones as well.

On the first floor of the building, there were some dozen shops - garments', electronic-goods', an STD booth, and two cyber cafés. On the opposite side of the road, there were some makeshift stalls - a barber shop, some tea-stalls. Beyond the large building there was a vacant field. At one corner of that field the old Exchange Office was standing. On the rest of that field a local realtor was constructing a housing complex; opposite the road, there was also a sweetmeat shop. The shopkeeper was casting alert look on each and every passer-by.

Sonai couldn't find Afjal in the club; then he went to the sweetmeat shop to ask the shopkeeper about Afjal, because the guy was a close aide of the latter.

Sonai whispered in his ear, "Where is Afjal?"

"In the office," the shopkeeper answered. Sonai walked few steps forward; and then turning right, he again walked a few steps down a narrow street, before stopping in front of a two-storied house.

This was the posh locality of Bibeknagar. The officials of various government departments, the local business men, the Circle Inspector of the local police station lived there. The ground floor of the building was transformed into an office for Salem's courier company. He had also opened another office at Kidderpore. As Sonai pushed the sliding door, a cool breeze greeted him. The room was luxuriously decorated with mahogany cabinets, murals, and gorgeous sofa sets. A rare piece of chandelier was hanging from the ceiling. Afjal was playing cards all by himself. A devilish smile was hovering on his thin lips. Sonai was so engrossed in his own thoughts that he didn't notice it. He told him anxiously, "Oh, Afjal! What did you do last night? You teased my sis!"

"I'm really sorry." Afjal replied with mock seriousness.

"I'm in great trouble, yaar. She has threatened me that she would tell father. I don't know what to do." Sonai's voice was fraught with sheer panic.

"Hide somewhere for few days. By that time your sister will have cooled off," Afjal advised him.

"But where shall I go?" Sonai asked helplessly.

"Go to Siliguri. It's a beautiful place," Afjal replied

carefully.

Sonai liked the suggestion and promptly left for home.

After Sonai's departure, Afjal quickly dialed Salem's number and informed him that Sonai would be going to Siliguri.

"Very good! Give him those packets. That takes care of one problem," Salem said cheerfully. "When is he going?" he asked further.

"He'll board a bus from Esplanade in the evening," informed Afjal.

Salem telephoned Saukat and informed him that a person named Sonai was going to Siliguri with the packets.

A convinced Sonai went home to collect his clothes. He told Pratima, "I'm going to Siliguri, mama."

"Who are going with you?" she asked.

"Some friends are going there. They are requesting me to accompany them."

"Won't you wait till your dad returns?"

"I've to start off right now, mama," he answered nervously.

Pratima didn't continue the conversation. She hurried towards the kitchen to bring some food for him. He embraced her from behind and said coaxingly, "Are you anxious, mama?"

"Yes, my love. I'll be worried until you return safely."

Pramath had gone to the market. She apprised him of Sonai's tour to Siliguri when he returned. Pramath felt sad when he heard that his son did not wait till his return. She understood that he was hurt; so she told him, "He fears you. He tells me that you are not happy with him."

"But I am always his well-wisher. He should know it," he said slowly as he was a bit upset.

"You're talking from a dad's pedestal," she answered.

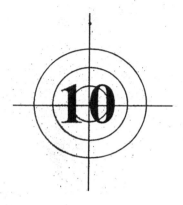

The previous night's experience was so agonizing for Mumpi that she wept bitterly for a long time. Next morning Pratima knocked at the door several times but she did not respond. Then she called Pramath, who banged on the door and said, "You know that your dad is a high blood pressure patient. Please, open the door."

Few minutes later Mumpi opened the door.

They asked her anxiously, "Are you all right?"

"Yes."

"Then why didn't you open the door?"

"Last night I caught a cold and my head was aching. I thought that a sound sleep will help me; so I popped a pill and fell fast asleep."

Pramath touched her on the forehead and exclaimed, "Oh, you've a fever! I must call in a doctor."

"Don't worry. It's only a slight one." She assured them with a faint smile.

"Tell your pampered daughter to have some breakfast. I'm going into the kitchen to prepare her favourite dish," Pratima told Pramath.

"Be a good girl and comply with your mom's request," he told Mumpi.

After breakfast Mumpi telephoned Afroj. "Can I meet you right now?" she asked him.

He was getting ready to go to office. He told her, "Today I've a busy schedule. I've to accompany some foreign delegates. But I'm telling my boss that I can't go. After all you're my first priority."

"No, no. Your boss will be angry," she said anxiously. But he reassured her and told her to come over.

On the southern part of Bibeknagar, lies a vast slum. This place is known as Tattunagar. When jute mills were built on the bank of the Ganga by the British before Independence, poor Muslims and Hindus from different states such as Bihar, Uttar Pradesh, Madhya Pradesh, and even from Andhra Pradesh of South India migrated there for bread and butter.

The whole place was more or less like a ghetto; the streets were broken muddy narrow; people would live in tiny rooms, packed like chickens. The daily life of those people would start with the siren of jute mills. After daylong labour in the mills, the men folk would come back home. Before their return the women folk would sit before the chullahs to make chapattis and dal. The glass bangles would creak as those busy hands would make dough. The red bindis on the foreheads would glow as the unruly fire would leap from the chullahs.

The children would while away the days on the lanes playing beside the kachcha drains that would emit obnoxious smell. The cows tethered beside the rooms would eat from the troughs nonchalantly as the women would milk them in the evening.

The sky would glow ash-white above the tiny lanes while the men would chat sitting on the charpoys- the topics were mainly the mills. Some of them would chant the Ramayana.

Apparently life was dull and drab for those people, but they were content as they had small demands from life. They were very happy when they could go back to the native villages; such trips would take place when there was an occasion of marriage, or festivals.

Another thing would also make them very excited- that was when someone would visit Kolkata. The whole neighbourhood would gather in that person's home to listen to his experiences in the City as if that person had returned from Paradise.

During 1970s, when the leftists started their anti-establishment gheraos, lock-outs and strikes, these jute mills crumbled down one by one. Those labourers that once flocked there for livelihood lost their jobs. Some went back home; some started hawking; others were engaged in begging and criminal activities. At that time wagon looting was a profitable profession for the antisocial elements.

Soon after that, the realty boom set in; and simultaneously the nature of crime also changed. Extortion of money, after kidnapping the owners of the handful industries that survived in the state, took place too frequently to scare other industrialists to venture into.

Poverty and lack of proper education stood in the way of the hopes and aspiration of the people of Tattunagar. Many of them were entangled in the murky activities of the local gangs that would engage those youths in crimes like extortion and smuggling. Moreover, these people were under the clutch of religious fundamentalists. The influence of the clerics upon them was immense, as they would follow the fatwa instead of the laws of the modern society. Many of them would secretly cherish Pakistan as their motherland and hoist Pakistan's flag during India-Pakistan match. After the demolition of the Babri Mosque, some sort of distrust was created between the Hindus and the Muslims, replacing the once-cherished feelings of tolerance and amicable sentiment.

The street where Afroj lived was named after the famous sultan of Karnataka, Haider Ali. When Mumpi reached his apartment, she saw that he was reading a newspaper, lying on the bed. He did not notice her; she wanted to surprise him; hence she went into the kitchen to brew two cups of coffee. Then placing them on a tray, she entered his bedroom and whispered in his ear, "Coffee, and me, sir". When he saw her, his eyes were filled with both joy and wonder.

He crooned, "Drink to me with only thy eyes, and I'll pledge no wine."

She leaned towards him with mock attention as if to listen to what he was crooning. Just then it seemed to him as if a rain-washed tuberose bent over him with all her fragrance. He felt an irresistible desire to kiss her. Sensing his intention, she tried to withdraw but by this time his arms had embraced her neck to pull her towards him.

"Don't be naughty," she reproached him, but it sounded very hollow as she lowered herself to meet his lips.

They decided to spend the whole day together. She told him, "I'll cook for you my favourite dishes. Go to market and buy some mutton. Today I'll try some new recipe."

Few years ago, when he started to court her, she had to think over his proposal very seriously. First of all, they belonged to different religions. Then her mom was dead against him. Also, she heard from her friends that they eat beef. When she expressed her anxiety over it, he roared with laughter. "Why are you laughing?" she was peeved.

"You're so childish. Beef is a nice food. Do you

know that the Europeans also eat beef?"

"I don't want to know who eats or who doesn't? But you can't eat it. That's all," she retorted.

After lunch Afroj took a short nap. Sitting beside him, she was leafing through a magazine; but actually, she was not reading; rather thinking about their first meeting. She had a friend, Rezina Khatoon. One day she went to Rezina's house to collect some class notes. Suddenly a storm started blowing and after it subsided, the rain began falling incessantly. When she came out of the house, she saw the lane was dark and deserted. Rezina told her that she would escort her to the main road, but she told her that she could go alone.

The neighbourhood was tangled in a net of serpentine lanes. She had to cross two lanes before arriving at the main road. When she crossed the second lane, she heard some footsteps behind her. Looking behind, she found some men were following her. She could sense their intention; she started running; but they soon caught her and were dragging her towards a deserted house. She was screaming hysterically. Suddenly, a man came out from a nearby house; those men panicked when they saw him and fled away.

He told her that his name was Afroj and he lived in that house. Then he escorted her to her house. She told him that she studied in the local college. Next day, when she was returning from college, she noticed that he was standing at the entrance of the college campus. When her look fell on him, he waved his hand to her, and hurried to her. Coming close he told her, "Hi, may I escort you to wherever you want to go?"

Remembering that, she heaved a sigh. "He is very responsible. He always takes care of my problems; mom still hates him so much. I cry out of despair, but he does not break down; rather he consoles me saying everything will be all right," she thought wistfully.

Afroj's grandfather Hanif was a resident of Ara district of Bihar. He had heard from Hanif that they were poor land labourers. When the jute mills were set up along the bank of the Ganga in Tattunagar, Hanif migrated there with his family. Hundreds of people like him migrated to Tattunagar for a better life and livelihood.

Afroj would love to hear stories of those days that Hanif would often tell him. The locality stretching from Bibeknagar to Tattunagar was divided into three parts: along the bank of the Ganga were the jute mills; thereafter a Hindu neighbourhood was set up; then came up the house of the Governor-General of India, the barracks, and a church; and finally, a Muslim muhallah was set up. Outside the periphery of the locality, there was a vast agricultural field. In-between was laid the railway tracks. A zoo was also set up beside the Governor's house where lions, tigers, hyenas, kangaroos - different types of animals- were kept. Once a tiger escaped from the cage and leapt on the road. People were going to the mills at that time. When they saw a tiger was prowling on the road, they ran helter-skelter in all directions; and as a result many people got caught in a stampede. Finally, the soldiers shot the tiger.

The British set up settlements for people of numerous professions. According to the professions of those people the localities were named like 'bazaz muhallah' (estate of cloth sellers), 'mochi muhallah' (estate of cobblers), 'kunjra muhallah' (estate of vegetables and fish mongers), and 'morga muhallah' (estate of chicken sellers). Every morning the soldiers would come to the market; and the locals could not enter the market before the soldiers.

Afroj heard from his grandfather that those days were very colourful, full of creativity, gracefulness, and discipline. Everyday the roads were washed with water that would come from the Ganga. When the Governor-General would visit Bibeknagar, in the afternoon he would ride an elephant to wander around the neighbourhood. The soldiers would march behind the elephant and the local people would gather on either side of the streets to watch the procession.

On the eastern side, in a remote place there lived an indigo planter William Lawful. He would patrol the solitary village path in search of beautiful local women. He would forcibly take them on his horseback and gallop to his house to rape them; an old village woman was his informer, providing him with news about the young pretty dames in the villages.

Again, Mumpi could remember an old incident. Three years ago her college arranged an excursion to Vizag. A Muslim family was also travelling in the same compartment. The bride was covered in burqa - only the eyes were open. Mumpi and her friends were laughing, chatting, pulling one other's legs; she suddenly noticed that those eyes were looking at them like a thirsty traveller in a desert. Later when Afroj telephoned her, she sobbed out, "Will you force me to wear burqa after marriage?" A confused Afroj asked her, why she was crying?

"Will you force me to wear a burqua?" she cried piteously.

They decided to watch a movie in the evening. When they reached the hall, the movie had already started. Afroj handed the tickets to the usher and said, "Back row, please." It was pitch-dark inside the hall. A young boy came sauntering down the aisle with a tray of popcorns and chips. "Will you take something?" Afroj asked.

Mumpi shrugged her shoulders. "Anything will do," she answered.

Most of the viewers were young couples who were not so eager to watch the movie; they came to spend intimate moments in comfortable darkness of the hall. When the movie ended, the clock struck half past ten. At first he escorted her home. When he reached his own neighbourhood, he saw that the whole muhallah was reeling from a severe power cut. The road was broken and spotted with countless potholes. He fell down in a pothole; as a result his right ankle was nastily bruised and he was limping.

The accident occurred only few yards away

from an old house. The door of that house was loosely closed. He pushed it gently to see that three suspicious guys were sitting around a table. A candle was flickering on the table. Those guys were so deep in conversation that the slight opening of the door escaped their attention. The guy who was sitting in the middle was talking to the others.

"Listen boys. We've got an order. If we can successfully carry it out then bhaiji will give us twenty thousand bucks," he told them. One could see the excitement on the faces of the guys.

"Have you got the contract for killing any big shot?" one guy asked.

"No. Tomorrow we've to steal a truck from the port of Kidderpore," the first guy informed him.

"What will we do if the police know about our plan and try to prevent us?" the other guys wanted to know.

"Bhaiji has ordered me to kill anyone who will get in the way. Remember that he'll not spare us if we fail," the first guy warned them about the grim consequence.

Afroj was listening to their conversation with so rapt attention that he could not feel that someone had come up behind him till a cold revolver touched the nape of his neck. A man ordered him to enter the room at gunpoint. The guys who were inside the room were stunned when they saw Afroj.

The man who caught Afroj told them, "When I

was coming here I found that he was spying on you."

The first guy shouted at Afroj, "Bastard!" Then he slapped Afroj so hard that Afroj fell on the ground; his cracked lips were oozing blood; he was stammering, "I…I…haven't done anything…please …leave me."

The man who was dangling the revolver kicked Afroj and said, "I can bet my dick that the son of a bitch is telling lies."

"Boss, what will we do with this asshole?" the other guys asked the first guy.

"Right now we've to start our operation; so at present tie up the bastard and dump him in some corner of the room," he ordered them.

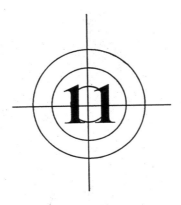

After stashing the RDX in the deserted house in Old Delhi, Moulavi came back to Bibeknagar. He was the cousin brother of the moulavi of the local mosque of Bibeknagar, but in real life he was a terrorist attached to the HuJI-B. He was so cautious that only Sher Khan and a few top leaders of the HuJI-B would know his real identity. Coincidentally, it was the mosque where he first met Salem, who frequented the worship place to find peace of mind.

That Moulavi had begun to watch him, Salem could not know for a long time.

Then one day Moulavi told Salem, "What ails you so much, my son? Tell me. I'll pray to Allah for you. He will certainly free you from your pain."

There was such magic in his tone that Salem was mesmerized, and he unfolded to him who he was. Moulavi listened to Salem intently because he was looking for exactly this type of person. He did not delay in goading Salem into the mission of Jihad. He used his charm and clever words, after selectively invoking religious text to convince Salem that he was doing the right thing.

For Moulavi it was an important task, as Salem became a dangerous criminal who spread his dirty tentacles under the protection of some local political leaders and a section of police officers. His men would fondly call him "M.L.A". Although he was not a real- life M.L.A (member of the legislative assembly), he was more powerful than any real one. During elections his men would cast bogus votes for his political patrons.

Salem was not a six-foot-tall brawny man with several cut marks on his body like a typical Bollywood villain. Those who saw him as a child confirmed that he was a whining baby during childhood. What was funny about him was his big sausage like face with a carrot like nose that would twitch spontaneously.

According to a report of the State Department of the U.S, the HuJI-B was formed by Fazlul Rahman, an associate of Osama bin Laden, who (Fazlul) joined bin Laden's World Islamic Front for the jihad against the Jews and the Crusaders in 1998. The HuJI-B aimed to establish harsh Islamic rule in Bangladesh by waging war against the progressive modern people. It raised a slogan: "We will become Taliban and turn Bangladesh into Afghanistan." This group reportedly recruits cadres from tens of thousands of madrasas in Bangladesh, allegedly spreading tentacles in numerous madrasas in West Bengal. The Rohingyas, who fled from Myanmar over the years due to religious persecution in Myanmar, have approximately 12 million people in Bangladesh, mainly in Chittagong. They are recruited by the HuJI-B. This organization runs many training camps in Bangladesh.

Intelligence reports of both the government of India and the U.S indicate that the ISI of Pakistan impart military training to the cadres of the HuJI-B, and the ULFA, and the KLO in the Kurigram and Rangapur areas of Bangladesh, near Coochbehar district of West Bengal and after training they sneak into West Bengal, to carry out subversive operations in other parts of the country. The apprehension of the intelligence department became true when the Asif Reja Commando Force attacked the American Centre in January 22, 2002. The arrest of Aftab Ansari alias Aftab Ahmed alias Farhan Malik, the prime accused in the attack exposed the link between the HuJI-B and the ISI, and the powerful base of the HuJI-B West Bengal, particularly in and around Kolkata.

Moulavi understood that Salem could be a potential instrument in their mission.

"This world is not the real world. The kafers believe that this world is the only world and what they receive through their perception is the true knowledge. But we, the sachcha Muslims, don't believe so; we know that the real world is beyond this illusion: that world is Allah's world. We have to be transported to that world, the ultimate abode of Allah. But this is not very easy as it requires strong determination to carry out Allah's Will. Anyone who will come in our way will be eliminated. Remember that you're not alone. Allah's servants are everywhere - in China, Pakistan, Bangladesh, Afghanistan, Russia, Uzbekistan, Holland, Romania, England, the U.S., everywhere," he told Salem.

Then he took Salem to Bangladesh to meet the leaders of the HuJI-B. At first they reached Narayanganj from Dhaka and from there they walked for thirty minutes on a kachcha road to reach a house. Salem was accommodated in a room. There were two more rooms in the house that were occupied by some youths. Later he came to know that they were the cadres of the insurgent organizations of north-east India like the NDFB, the NSCN (K), the ULFA, and the KLO.

Next day, at about five in the morning, two jeeps arrived there. One of them was already occupied by five army officers who were speaking in Urdu. Salem and the others boarded the other jeep. They crossed Faridpur at about half past eight and after another half an hour's journey, they reached a desolate place. Their eyes were blindfolded before the jeep started running again. It took an hour's journey when they reached a camp. The camp was used as a training ground of sophisticated arms. There Salem met some persons who were obviously important in the organization, though they did not disclose their identity. They decided to use him as a local base for stacking arms in and around Kolkata. According to the intelligence report of the U.S State Department, this terrorist organization would receive arms from the ISI and these arms would reach them from clandestine places of Myanmar and Thailand and would arrive at the port of Cox's Bazaar via sea route. Then they would hand over those arms to the ULFA, the NSCN, and other insurgent groups through the porous border of Meghalaya.

This state, fondly called "the abode of clouds", is torn with the daily atrocities by these terrorist groups. It has seven administrative districts; five of them share a common border with Bangladesh. The Garo Hills, due to ruggedness, are used by the terrorists to smuggle arms. The smuggled arms are sent to Assam by road for the ULFA.

Sometimes arms were smuggled through the porous border between the Coochbehar sector comprising Jalpaiguri and Coochbehar districts, and Bangladesh. The 410 kilometres of international border with Bangladesh has NH31 and NH31A and broad gauge and metre gauge railway lines running through West Bengal before entering Assam. The demographic character within the five kilometre belt of the border with Bangladesh underwent rapid changes with the heavy influx of the Bangladeshi people, settling there.

Arms were smuggled in trucks that would ply to and from Bangladesh carrying goods. These arms were hidden in some madrasas and then were transported to various places.

Since the quantity of arms smuggled through the West Bengal-Bangladesh border was not huge due to constant vigil of the Border Security Forces and the route via the Garo Hills to Assam to Siliguri to Kolkata was long and hence risky, this time the ISI took an adventurous step to use the port of Kidderpore for arms consignments. It was highly risky, but at the same time huge amount of arms might have been sent through these shipments.

"Choose a man who can do it," Sher Khan ordered Moulavi.

"I know a man who can do it," Moulavi answered. He told him about Salem. Sher Khan was impressed and told Moulavi to engage Salem. Moulavi told Salem to open an export-import business. Salem was converted into a garment merchant. In Kidderpore he opened a garment factory which was obviously a cover-up while the real operation was going on to bring arms.

The port of Kidderpore was built up by the East India Company after getting grants from the Mughal Emperor to carry on business transaction. The port's importance was immense keeping in view the vast hinterland that it commands, including the whole East and North East region, Bihar, and the neighbouring countries like Bhutan and Nepal.

The loading and unloading of cargos from the containers was controlled by the local mafia. The security arrangement was not tight, technically it was level one, which meant it was just ordinary security. The customs checking was not very strict. Salem befriended some customs officers who would clear his containers without checking and in return, they would receive hefty pay packets.

The modus operandi was that Afjal would bring out the truck from port and stash it in Salem's factory at Kidderpore. Then those arms would have been sent to various terrorist organizations through his courier company that was launched solely for that purpose.

Swaroop Jain was a businessman, whose brother-in-law, Vijay, was a broker in a clearing agency at Kidderpore and he convinced Swaroop to open such a clearing agency.

"It's very profitable business," he advised Swaroop. After initial hesitation, Swaroop opened "Shiva Clearing Agency & Co".

Vijay looked after the business as he had some previous experience. When Salem started his garments' business, Swaroop was appointed his clearing agent. When linen would come from Bangladesh or Tanzania, Salem would give Swaroop the authorizing letter to clear the goods from the dock.

Manish Jain joined Shiva Clearing Agency & Co only three months ago. Swaroop was affectionate towards Manish as he was also a Jain, and secondly, Manish was very honest. Once Manish lent two 40-foot- tall containers to a business man in Nepal, who never returned them. The case was still pending in the High Court. After that bitter experience, he became very cautious.

It was the 3rd of November when the Aegean Glory arrived at the port of Kidderpore. The gangway was attached to the deck of the ship while derricks were ready to pull the gigantic containers from the ship. The containers were safely offloaded on the ground. The customs officer and the clearing agent were informed.

When the arms consignment arrived at the port, Manish checked the papers. He saw that some bales of linen were waiting to be cleared. When the bales were being loaded onto the truck, one bale slipped from the hand of a labourer and fell on the ground with a thud. Manish thought he heard the sound of some hard metal banging against the inside wall of the bale. Manish knew that linen could not produce such a sound. The customs officer who was checking the bales also heard the sound; but when Manish asked him, "Sir, have you heard the sound of some metal?" the officer flatly denied.

"Sir, there must be something else inside the container," Manish repeated.

But the officer was exasperated. "It's all right," he answered with an angry look.

Manish didn't dare insist.

Later, in the office, he talked to Swaroop on that matter, but he also said, "Never mind."

Salem was informed that his goods had been loaded onto the truck and it was waiting in the terminus.

When Afroj arrived at the old house, Afjal and his men were drawing up a plan to bring the truck out from the port. After dumping Afroj in the old house, they arrived at Salem's factory at Kidderpore. Salem told Afjal to take two men to the port next day in the morning and bring the consignment to the factory.

They reached the port at nine in the morning. The guards did not stop them at the gate as they would often enter the port as Salem's workers. When they were a quarter of a mile away from the truck terminus, Afjal noticed the place was unusually calm and quiet; the usual din and bustle was absent. Some porters were casually walking to and fro. He looked around carefully but nothing unnatural came in sight. Some trucks were standing under a shade. Afjal ordered his men to read the number plates; the white letters seemed as mysterious as ever. The truck for which they came was standing right in the middle.

The border between India and Bangladesh is the most vulnerable as there is not any practical demarcation line between these two neighbouring countries. The demarcation made by the Radcliff Line was on paper; hence there are many houses on the border whose front doors are in India and the backsides are in Bangladesh. The boundary line touches five states of India including West Bengal, Tripura, Manipur, Assam, and Mizoram and it is the longest boundary line that India has with any of her neighbours, measuring approximately 3436 kilometers in length.

There are approximately 100 villages that are on zero line at the boundary and more than 100 enclaves measuring approximately 17,158 acres that belong to India are actually in Bangladesh and more than 50 enclaves, measuring approximately 7,110 acres, though belong to Bangladesh, are actually in India. The actual figures are not available; however to sort out the problem a joint Indo-Bangladesh border working group was set up, as the Land Boundary Agreement between two countries in 1974 laid down procedures for solving border disputes ;but the problem still persists.

The geographical features of West Bengal and Bangladesh are so similar that any one can intrude into West Bengal from Bangladesh, quite easily. Although the border fencing work is going on, there are many points from where anybody can enter into West Bengal.

The border between India and Bangladesh can be compared with that of the US and Mexico in terms of illegal import of arms and drugs. But India-Bangladesh border is unique because it poses a grave threat to India's internal security, as the ISI-sponsored terrorists sneak into India with arms and reach Delhi and Mumbai to carry out subversive activities. The confession of several terrorists arrested by anti-terrorist squads in Mumbai and Delhi proves it; besides, huge amount of fake Indian currency notes are also being imported into India through this porous border to ruin the economy of India.

Saukat crossed the border through a tiny village.

He was going to meet the leaders of the terrorists, but a farmer noticed him while he was crossing the border and informed the jawans posted at the nearby post. Saukat boarded a bus to reach Phuentsholing in Bhutan- his destination was a hotel where the terrorists would wait for him. Being tipped off by the farmer, the security personnel followed him and caught him from the bus.

The Border Security Forces' camp was witnessing a flurry of activity. Top officials from Kolkata had arrived at the camp after the arrest of Saukat. During interrogation Saukat revealed that he was an active member of the HuJI-B. Further, he disclosed that huge arms were scheduled to arrive at the port of Kidderpore and then those arms and ammunition would be sent to different terrorist organizations.

When the Chief Secretary Vijay Singh received the information from North Block, he rang the Commissioner of Kolkata Police Anil Sen and the Chief of the state intelligence bureau Praful Sinha. The trio decided to send a special team to the port to find the truck.

The Chief Secretary had insisted that the Police Commissioner choose one of his most efficient officers for the operation. The Commissioner called in six young officers and told them, "Some terrorists will try to swipe a truck from the port. They have to be intercepted, but remember that we want them alive." While other officers were hesitating, Bikramjeet Banerjee came forward and said, "Sir, I'm ready to take the onus."

"Very good! Remember you will talk to me only during the operation."

After arriving at the port, Bikramjeet ordered the constables to take positions. The gates were kept open so that the terrorists could not sense anything wrong.

When Afjal and his men got on the truck and started the engine, the police came out from their hiding. Bikramjeet ordered them to surrender, but Afjal drove the truck crashing the front gate. When it became evident that Afjal was running away with the truck, Bikramjeet ordered his men to follow the truck. He drove his jeep towards the truck and aimed his revolver at the driver's seat and opened firing. A bullet smashed the windscreen and pierced the right armpit of Afjal, who felt a deadly pain benumbed his senses. He could not hold the steering wheel any longer and slid from the driver's seat and then fell on the right side of the floor of the truck. Fresh blood coming out from his wound made a little puddle on the floor.

A constable fired at the tyres of the truck to stop it, but it could not bear the thrust of its own speed and overturned. As a result two aides of Afjal were killed on the spot. Afjal was rushed to hospital but his condition was deteriorating very fast. Anil Sen himself arrived at the hospital to record the confession of Afjal, but "Sonai Siliguri arms" were the final words that Afjal uttered.

The seizure included 3,000 kg of RDX, 20

SMG rifles, 400 hand grenades, 360 LMG rounds, 50 explosive detonators, 300 AK47s and 50,000 rounds of ammunition.

Nicholas and the crew of the ship were arrested and a team of intelligence officers interrogated them. Nicholas pretended that he did not know English; hence an interpreter who knew Latvian was called up to the interrogation chamber. Nicholas told them that the ship was owned by an Arab tycoon of Tanzania and they set out from the port of Dar es Salaam. The ship was carrying sugar, tea, tobacco, and linen.

The police raided the office of Salem and seized many important documents. The officers also detained Swaroop.

At that time Manish approached the officers. "Sir, I want to tell something," he told them nervously. The officers could not guess what important clue Manish could provide them. He narrated everything from the arrival of the cargo ship to the reaction of the customs officer.

Meanwhile, some other officers were studying the documents that were seized from Salem's office. They found that a particular company in Dhaka would often get order from Salem to send cotton.

The matter was immediately referred to Rajat, who instructed an officer posted at the Indian High Commission in Dhaka to find out the company. The seized documents revealed that the Bangladesh-based company had an office in Dhaka.

The officer found that the address was a fake one; in fact, there was no existence of such an office. After some investigation by that RAW officer it was revealed that the office was actually a cover-up of the HuJI -B.

In the meantime the logbook of the ship that the officers seized showed that a company from Tanzania was sending the linen and the recipient was Salem's company. Nicholas was brought to the headquarters of the intelligence department. Rajat flew from New Delhi to interrogate him. He was accompanied by two senior RAW officers.

The interrogation chamber was a high ceiling bare room, plastered with dull white coat, with no window and completely sound proof. A long table was laid at the centre of the room. A powerful bulb hanging from the ceiling provided the only source of light in the room. The constables brought Nicholas to the room and made him sit on a chair facing the officers. The interpreter was brought in who could understand Latvian.

Nicholas was visibly very tired as the officers were interrogating him continuously for the last three days. He could hardly sleep an hour during those days. The officers were asking him repeatedly the same question, "Who send those arms?"

Earlier, he would answer doggedly, "I don't know."

But he broke down finally under the tremendous psychological pressure.

"Who told you to bring those arms?" asked Rajat. Nicholas looked at him laboriously. The high voltage light was focused on his face. He could feel the sheer heat; he could not bear it any longer.

"I want to sleep," he moaned.

"Of course, we'll let you sleep. But before that you've to tell us who sent those arms," Rajat said sternly.

"I'm speaking the truth. I don't know him. We've met only once," Nicholas confessed at last, "In a hotel in Brussels. He gave me dollars and asked me to transport the arms to Kidderpore Port."

"Where those arms were loaded?"

"At the mouth of the Karnaphuli River. The arms were loaded from a speedboat that came from Myanmar," Nicholas gave the details.

From the description provided by Nicholas a police artist sketched the mysterious man who had influenced him to despatch arms to the port of Kidderpore. Rajat whistled in disbelief when he saw the sketch of Sher Khan, whose method of operation was deadly. When he would launch an operation, he would use two routes to reach the goal, so that if a route was blocked, then the alternative route was used to achieve the objective. He pushed many agents inside the Bangladesh Liberation Army who would tip off the Pakistani Army about their plans. As a result many cadres of the Liberation Army were killed in sudden ambush. He also killed many civilians, including students and intellectuals.

RAW tried to capture him; but after the war was over, nobody heard about him. When the Pakistani Army surrendered to the Indian Army, Indian intelligence officers searched for him, but he just vanished. Some thought he was killed, but his dead body was never found. The file on Sher Khan was sent to RAW archive as classified information.

Rajat requested the state police to send him the file on Salem. He found it very important. He was sure Salem was used in the operation, but he was also certain that Salem was not the man that had direct link with Sher Khan or the ISI.

But who was that missing link? He was certain that the person was hiding somewhere, waiting for an opportunity to strike. The immediate thought that came in his mind was to check the borders of Rajasthan and Gujarat if some explosives already came from Pakistan. RAW agents began to interrogate the smugglers, but none could give any clue.

The airports were put on high alert; but nothing dubious was found.

The smugglers could not give any clue because Nasir, who brought the RDX from Pakistan, was not a known face in the racket. The ISI found him luckily. He had a cousin brother in Pakistan who visited India when the Samjhauta Express was launched between India and Pakistan. That cousin brother was an ISI agent, who came to Jaipur to meet Nasir at the behest of the ISI. He told Nasir that he would get a huge amount of money if he could do the job. Nasir readily agreed as he was a greedy bloke.

The ISI and the HuJI-B were not sitting inactive. Sher Khan ordered the leaders of the HuJI-B to send some suicide bombers who could kill Saukat because if Rajat could have wrested out Moulavi's name from Saukat, then the total game plan would have been exposed. Three suicide bombers sneaked into North Bengal whose target was to reach Saukat at any cost and kill him. Saukat was arrested by the Border Security Forces; but next day a team of West Bengal police took charge of him and they were bringing him to Kolkata in a prison van. On the way they were attacked by those suicide bombers who used so powerful bombs that the van and the men inside it were blown into pieces.

Meanwhile, Moinak Chatterjee, the executive assistant of the secretary of the ruling party, received the phone call that came from the Chief Minister's residence. The secretary Amal Bose, who was sleeping at that time got angry and cried out, "Idiot! Why have you broken my sleep?" But when Moinak informed him that the CM Ajit Pradhan was on the line, he hastily got down from the bed to receive the call. Ajit narrated the whole incident and requested him to call in at his residence.

Amal's friends would call him Chanakya because he had the power to solve any crisis, however difficult; but this time the situation was very sensitive.

Ajit was a person who would get nervous at

the slightest touch of allegation against him. He told Amal nervously, "You know the hawks in the press. I'm sure that they'll soon get the news and then they'll leave no stone unturned to malign me. I can imagine what tomorrow's headlines would be."

Amal would know very well the nature of Ajit; so he let him babble out till he stopped. Then he told Anil Sen, "You will hand out a press release about how your police department killed some terrorists and rescued a truck full of arms and ammunition."

"Sir, shall we arrest Salem?" Anil asked him.

"Yes."

Salem had been continuously in contact with Afjal by a mobile phone. When Afjal realised that the police had laid a trap for them, he immediately informed Salem. Without any delay Salem drove fast towards Basirhat, a border town of West Bengal. The border was very porous and he would know many secret places from where he would cross the border and enter into Bangladesh.

When the police raided his house, he was heading fast to Narayanganj in Bangladesh to reach the headquarters of the HuJI-B.

On the 3rd of November, Sonai boarded a
Siliguri-bound express bus from Esplanade. Afjal
came with him at the bus stop. When the bus started
moving, he gave Sonai a card box and two packets
and said, "There are some books in these packets.
Here is the address of the man who lives on Hill Cart
Road. Please give him the packets."

When the bus was leaving the depot, a youth
scampered into the bus. The conductor told him to
sit beside Sonai. "This damn traffic jam of Kolkata,"
he remarked, smiling at Sonai, as if he wanted Sonai
to support him. Sonai nodded approvingly.

Some people in this world can't travel without
speaking continuously. Perhaps this youth belonged
to that class.

"Going to Siliguri or dropping on the way?" he
asked Sonai, thumping on the seat.

"Siliguri," Sonai replied.

"So am I. I've a trade there. Liquor, you know," he winked.

"Oh! That's great," Sonai tried to be polite.

"Nothing remarkable, you know. Do you stay there?" The youth was inquisitive.

"It's my first visit," informed Sonai.

"I'm Robin. What's your name?" the youth deftly tried to know Sonai's name and destination.

"Sonai Biswas," Sonai replied, not knowing the ulterior motive of the youth.

"Glad to meet you," Robin extended his hand towards Sonai.

Sonai could not suspect anything wrong about Robin.

At Dalkhola the bus stopped for half an hour, so that the passengers could respond to nature's call and could also get some food in some dhaba. Sonai noticed that someone snapped his photo but before he could catch the mysterious photographer, the man slipped away behind a crowd.

Next morning the bus reached Siliguri. Sonai got down from the bus. That nosy passenger Robin departed stealthily. "Strange fellow!" Sonai thought to himself.

At the roadside he saw the signboard of a hotel - the Blue Diamond. He remembered that Afjal told him to stay there. He entered the lobby of the hotel.

Some people were sitting on a sofa. Sonai booked a single room; entering the room, he switched on the light and sat on the bed.

Few minutes later a boy came to ask if he would like to give order for lunch. After the boy's exit, he bolted the door from inside. He wanted to have a shower; so he unzipped the bag to take out soap and a towel. He went to the bathroom and standing under the shower, began to lather himself. Suddenly the soap slipped from his hand on the floor. As his face was smeared with the foam of the soap, he could not see it and unfortunately stepped on it and slipped across the floor. As a result his head rammed against the wall. A cut mark appeared on his forehead. He groped inside the bag to bring out a piece of fresh cloth, so that he could put it on the wound to stop bleeding. Unfortunately, his fingers, already smeared with blood, touched one of the packets that he had to deliver. He felt very nervous when he saw what he had done.

He thought to himself, "Shit! I've spoilt the packet. Certainly, it would make them angry if I don't change the packet."

Putting on a dress he went to a nearby drug store. There a man behind the counter examined his wound and said, "Don't worry. It's only a minor cut." That man poured some tincture iodine on a piece of fresh cotton and pressed it on the wound and taped two Band Aids on it. After that Sonai went to a shop and bought some wrappers and ribbons. Returning hotel, he sat on the bed and placed the packets and wrappers and ribbons in front of him. Slowly he opened the blood stained packet; a chill shiver passed through his spine. He felt that his whole body was wet with perspiration; his heart was laden with some deadweight, as a revolver was staring at him and its steel body was mocking at him. Hastily, he opened the other packet and the card box and to his utter horror, found another revolver and the card box full of bullets!

His mind started working overtime. "I've been trapped by some terrorists. Now, if I go to the police, they won't believe me; on the other hand these people are so powerful that they will easily come to know that I've gone to the police. Then they will kill me. Better I feign that I know nothing and wait for them. But that's impossible. How can I hide my anxiety? They'll certainly read it on my face," he thought.

Finally, he decided to leave the packets and the card box in the room and escape from the hotel. He hid the revolvers and the bullets under the bed and came to the reception desk. The receptionist was talking to someone on the telephone. Sonai interrupted him and said, "Get my bill, please. I've to leave at once."

Outside the hotel he found a tiny shop whose owner was busy stacking empty bottles of soft drinks into the crates.

"Is there any other hotel here? Sonai asked him.

"Why are you asking this question? Is this not good one?" The shopkeeper was curious.

"The room service is very bad," Sonai told the lie.

"There is another hotel the Sunrise, which is half an hour's drive from here," the man replied.

Sonai noticed that the man was watching him sceptically. He didn't dare wait there.

Luckily, an autorickshaw was coming down the street. He stopped it and told the driver to take him to the hotel Sunrise. There he booked a room and locked himself in the room. He decided to pass the day in the hotel room and then to return home at night.

Half-hour later, after the departure of Sonai from the Blue Diamond, two men appeared at the hotel lobby. One of them asked the receptionist, "Has Mr. Sonai Biswas checked in?"

"He did but half an hour ago he checked out," replied the receptionist.

"Did he tell you where he was going?" they asked. Naturally, the receptionist could not inform them, as Sonai did not inform him.

When they discovered that Sonai had fled, they contacted their chief who ordered them to find him at any cost. They went to the shop outside the Blue Diamond and showed the owner Sonai's photo. The man confirmed that Sonai boarded an autorickshaw. Then they went to the autostand to find out the driver whose autorickshaw Sonai had boarded. They entered the drivers' room and showed the photo. A driver told them that he had taken Sonai to the hotel

Sunrise. They contacted their boss again to inform him that they had traced Sonai. He ordered them to kidnap him and bring him to their hideout.

They arrived at the hotel Sunrise and showed the photo to the receptionist. One of them whispered something in the ear of the receptionist. Instantly, the guy stood up in fear and with trembling feet led them to the room where Sonai was staying and pressed the doorbell. As soon as Sonai opened the door they entered the room, pushing him inside.

He cried out, "Who the hell are you?" but could not finish the sentence, as he was staring at the revolvers pointed at him. They walked him to a black car, parked outside the hotel and forced him to enter it.

Sonai's skedaddle from the Blue Diamond and two suspicious persons' enquiry about him raised doubt in the mind of the hotel receptionist who called in that boy and asked him, "Did you notice anything wrong when you went to room number13?"

"He was bleeding when I went to take the lunch order. He asked me about some medical store." the boy answered. Then suddenly, as if something had flashed through his mind, he cried out, "Oh, there were some packets on the bed."

"There must be something fishy about this man," the receptionist thought.

He unlocked the door of the room and started examining the drawers, the cupboards and the wastepaper basket. Finally, he leaned downwards to look under the bed. There he discovered those packets and the card box. He informed the police immediately.

Opening those packets and the card box, the police found two revolvers and bullets. They suspected that Sonai and those two men were terrorists who came to the hotel for the arms deal, but escaped leaving the revolvers and the bullets in the hotel room, because they feared that the police could raid the hotel any time. The commissionaire of the hotel informed them that the two suspects came in a black car. The police found the car in the forest of Hasimara.

The terrorists drove Sonai towards the deep dense forest of duars. They drove up to Hasimara and then entered into the jungle. There they left the car and took a trail through the jungle. In the afternoon they reached the foot of a hill. They began climbing the hill.

Since Sonai had no previous experience of climbing, he was soon on his knees and panting desperately with his head sunk between his legs. When his abductors saw that he could walk no further, they put up a tent to pass the night.

At dawn they again started their trek towards their camp. When they were very close to the camp, they heard that some doves were cooing. One of his abductors also started cooing. Few minutes' later four guards appeared before them in olive-coloured uniforms. They talked to the abductors and then tied the eyes of Sonai with a piece of cloth. He felt that they were leading him through a circuitous path. Finally, they stopped him and opened his eyes. He saw that he was standing before a scary looking man who told him, "You have betrayed us; so your punishment is death."

Afroj was tied to a chair and his mouth was stuffed with a large piece of cotton. A musty smell was floating in the room. From one corner of the room a spider was watching him sitting on a cobweb that was hanging from the ceiling. Although the goons put out the light of the room, a streak of light seeped into the room through the partly opened window frames. The goons kept him beside a rusty steel almirah. He would know pretty well that they would kill him as soon as they would come back after accomplishing their operation; hence he had to escape before they returned.

He stood up with a great effort and walked towards the door. The goons had locked the door from outside. He shoved the door with the chair that was tied to his back. "Bang! Bang!" the sound spread outside; but none came to his rescue because the whole locality was fast asleep. He was very tired and breathing heavily; so he decided to continue his efforts at dawn.

At four o'clock in the morning he began to shove the door with renewed efforts. For an hour nothing happened. At 5 a.m. a rickshaw puller who was passing there noticed that someone was pushing the door from inside.

He banged on the door and hollered, "Is anybody inside?"

Afroj increased the intensity of pushing but could not respond as his mouth was stuffed with cotton. The man came beside the only window of the house to check if it was open. When he found that the sound was growing louder, he was confident that somebody was locked inside. The window was closed from inside but there was a slight aperture between the two frames of the window. The man inserted a stick through the window and bent the stick with pressure to enlarge the gap. When the aperture became as big as a one-rupee coin, he put his eye on it to peep inside.

As soon as he found that a person was tied to a chair, he understood that the person had been kidnapped. Immediately, he informed the police who swung into action, breaking into the house and rescuing Afroj.

The officer at the Bibeknagar police station soon realised that Afroj's capture had a definite link with the port raid. He informed the headquarters.

The Special Investigation Team which was handling the case was very confused about the specific destination of Sonai. Before death, Afjal could only tell them that Sonai was sent with arms to Siliguri.

Moreover, they had no photograph or address of Sonai. In the meantime Darjeeling police informed Bikramjeet that they could seize two revolvers and a card box full of bullets from a room in the Blue Diamond and a person named Sonai Biswas had carried those arms and bullets in the hotel. Bikramjeet met Anil Sen and said, "Sir, I want to go to Bibeknagar because Darjeeling police could track down the whereabouts of Sonai from the hotel register." He was given the required permission; and Bikramjeet ordered the officer at Bibeknagar police station to pick up Sonai's father.

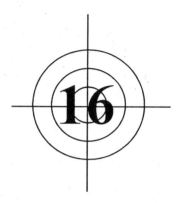

16

Pramath had been feeling blue and was lying long hours on bed in the morning. "I dreamt an ominous dream last night. Have you got any news from Sonai?" Pramath asked Pratima.

At that moment somebody banged on the front door violently.

·She went downstairs to see who the visitor was. As soon as she opened the door a posse of police dashed into the house. Quite perplexed by this sudden intrusion, she cried out, "Who're you?"

The sub-inspector who was leading the posse shouted gruffly, "Where is your husband? We've come here to arrest the bastard."

"Why are you talking rudely about my husband?

What has he done?" she protested.

"He has done nothing, but your son is helping the terrorists. Last night we arrested some of them. We have wrenched out the name of your son from them," the sub-inspector howled.

"It can't be true. You are making a huge mistake," she cried out.

"This is what everyone says at first. We've come with a search warrant," he said.

He went upstairs while the other policemen spread out into the house. Hearing the noise, Pramath got up from bed to see what was going on, but before he could go downstairs, the sub-inspector entered into the room. Pramath was highly astonished at seeing a policeman in his room but before he could utter any single word the sub-inspector asked him, "Is Sonai your son?"

"Yes, but what's the matter?" Pramath asked, being confused.

"Where is he?" the sub-inspector asked again.

"He has gone to Siliguri. But why are you asking it?" Pramath wanted to know.

"When did he go?"

"Two days ago. I'm asking you again, officer, what's the matter."

"Do you know why has he gone to Siliguri?"

"Why, can't he go on a tour?"

"Pooh! Nice story. He has gone there to deliver arms to the terrorists. You have to come with us."

He handcuffed Pramath and brought him to the police station. When Pramath arrived at the police station, he found that Afroj was sitting there. "Uncle, you here!"

Afroj was very surprised to see him.

"They are saying that my son is involved in illegal arms consignment delivery," Pramath answered.

"What nonsense!" Afroj shouted angrily.

The officer-in-charge interrupted their conversation.

"Do you know each other?" he asked them.

"I know him very well. He's an army officer," Afroj informed the officer.

The inspector got up from his chair and saluted Pramath. He told the officer who handcuffed Pramath to unlock the handcuff and reproached him.

"I was caught by some local antisocial elements. They tied me and then dumped me inside a house that they would use as their meeting place, but outside they put up a club's signboard. They were talking about a truck full of arms and ammunition. The truck was stationed at the port of Kidderpore," Afroj told Pramath.

In the evening Bikramjeet arrived at the police station.

"Sir, I have detained that person, but he is an army

officer," the officer told him.

"We need a room for interrogation," Bikramjeet said.

"Certainly, Sir. I have made all arrangements in my office."

They interrogated Pramath for three hours but he couldn't help them in this regard. Then Bikramjeet showed Pramath a sketch of a youth and asked, "Is he your son?"

When Pramath saw the sketch of his son, a fear of some unknown danger clutched him. "Where is my son? What have you done to him? I won't spare you if you do anything to him," he shouted anxiously.

"Cool down. We have done nothing to him," Bikramjeet replied.

"But where is he?"

"Do you know that your son is associated with the terrorists? He would supply them with arms."

"What nonsense! I don't believe it."

"We've seized two revolvers and bullets from a hotel room where he had lodged. But before we could nab him, he was rescued by his friends."

"If it is true I'll help you to arrest him."

Then Bikramjeet grilled Afroj.

"Your name?" he asked Afroj.

"Afroj."

"How did they catch you?"

"I went to see a film with my girlfriend. After the film was over, I escorted her home. Here I would like to mention that she is this gentleman's daughter. After that I was returning to my home. When I entered my muhallah, suddenly the power went off. I was hardly a few steps away from an old house when I fell down in a pothole and my right ankle got a serious bruise."

Afroj pulled the trouser over his right ankle to show the bruise to Bikramjeet, who eyed the bruise thoughtfully. Then he asked, "What happened next?"

"I went to the house to seek help. The door was partly closed. I overheard an excited conversation about a truck in the port area."

"How many of them were present there?" Bikramjeet interrupted.

"They were altogether three."

"Can you identify them?" Bikramjeet asked.

"Of course!"

Bikramjeet showed him the photos of Afjal and his two aides.

"These very guys were talking about stealing a truck. I swear I've seen them in the house," Afroj cried out in excitement.

"What were they discussing?"

"They were saying that the truck was full of arms which they would swipe."

"Did they say anything else?"

"Yes. They were talking about a local mafia don who gave them the order."

"What's his name?"

"Salem."

Pramath was listening to the interrogation.

Now, he asked Bikramjeet, "Do you have any idea where they could have taken Sonai?"

"We have information that they have gone into the forests of Bhutan. The car they were travelling had been found out by the police in the forest of Hasimara. We are suspecting that perhaps they are staying in Pasaka - just on the other side of the border."

At night when Pramath returned home with the news that the police were suspecting that Sonai was linked with the terrorists, Pratima burst into anger.

"You are a fool to believe them. Remember I won't spare you if my son does not return home safely," she shouted.

"Why are you accusing dad? Do you think dad is responsible? Besides why are you repeating 'my son'? We are all anxious for him!" Mumpi told Pratima.

Next day a reporter from a local newspaper visited their house. "I would like to know what actually happened to your son so that I can convey the truth to everyone," he told them.

"The police are investigating the case. So I can't say anything," Pramath said.

"At present it is not sub-judice," argued the reporter.

At that time Pratima interrupted Pramath and asked the reporter, "What do you want to know?"

"According to the police statement your son is associated with terrorists. Is it true?" the reporter asked her.

The question upset Pratima and she started sobbing. Mumpi consoled her mother, "You see, mama, God is great. He'll certainly save him." She wiped her mama's eyes.

Mumpi cast a sad smile at the reporter and said, "I can tell you everything, but it's a long story. Do you have the patience to listen to it?"

"Of course, I'll listen to. Is it not true that your brother was linked with Afjal and he would work in Salem's courier company?" the reporter repeated the earlier question.

"He would not mix with the local boys. So it was not possible for him to know who was antisocial and who was not."

"But is it possible that police will frame an innocent guy?" the reporter expressed his doubt.

"The real culprit is Salem. He has links with the terrorists. The local people know it very well, but everybody fears him because he is very powerful. It is also alleged that he helps some local leaders during elections," Mumpi replied.

"Isn't it true that your brother worked in Salem's courier's company?" the reported asked again.

"It's absolutely preposterous and fabricated by the media and the police. The police have concocted this story to hide their failure," Mumpi said.

Before leaving, the reporter said, "We'll publish it because people should know the truth."

Next day the report was published.

That evening, when they were sitting in the drawing room, they heard some people shouting angrily outside the house. Before they could realise what was going on, some hooligans stormed into the drawing room, armed with sticks, rods and swords. The leader was brandishing a revolver and was shouting "Break everything".

One thug rushed to a corner of the room where the replica of Rodin's 'The Thinker' was kept. He raised it upwards and threw it on the ground with a bang. It broke into pieces. Some others started breaking the glass windows and the beautiful paintings that Pramath's dad had collected from various art galleries. When Pramath saw that they were destroying those rare collections, he could not restrain himself and tried to snatch the paintings from their hands. One of them hit him on his head with an iron rod. He fell down on the floor like an uprooted tree. Blood oozed from the wound and his whole face was soon smeared.

The thug who was dangling the revolver bent over him and said in a menacing voice, "This is the first lesson for speaking against us. Next time we'll abduct your beautiful daughter. When we return her, you'll not be able to recognize her." Then he ordered his men to march out of the house.

Next day, when Pramath went to the market, a fish-seller whom he would know for the last twenty-five years asked him, "Is it true that your son has gone to the forest to get training from the terrorists?"

"Who has told you this nonsense?" Pramath shouted in anger.

"Everyone knows," replied the fish-seller. Pramath saw that other buyers were whispering "terrorist's father".

He could bear it no longer. He shouted at the extreme pitch of his voice, "Who dares to call my son a terrorist? If you have the guts, arrest Salem and his patrons, the political leaders, who have made my son a scapegoat." He left the market without buying anything.

Pratima was very surprised when she saw that he came back with an empty bag and became very upset when he told her what happened in the market. "I'm so scared for all of you," she told him.

That evening a phone call came when Mumpi was working in the computer centre. Pratima received the call. Her whole body was shivering in a nameless fear when the caller said, "We know your daughter has gone to the computer centre. We can kidnap her now." The receiver slipped away from her hand. The hanging receiver was still emitting that ominous voice. She wanted to call her husband, but her voice was choked. Pramath was astonished when he saw her.

"What's the matter?" he asked anxiously.

"Someone telephoned that he'll kidnap Mumpi," she cried.

"What are you talking?" Pramath sprinted to her side.

"We've to contact her at once; but I'm not finding the number," she was trembling in fear.

"Give it to me." He snatched the diary from her and found the number. When Mumpi received the call, he told her, "O, dear, are you okay! Don't leave office. I'll pick up you."

After the phone call they felt that the house was no longer safe for their daughter. Pratima requested her brothers to shelter her daughter; but they told her, "We can't do that. Our social position has already been damaged because of your son."

That night Pramath was sitting in an armchair on the roof. His eyes were closed. A storm was going on in his mind. The entire world was accusing his son of being a terrorist, but his mind was not ready to accept it.

Mumpi tiptoed to her dad and held his hand

firmly. He did not open his eyes, but realised that his daughter was beside him. They remained silent, but each knew what was going on in the other's mind. At last she broke the silence and said, "Don't worry, dad. Almighty God will protect him from all sorts of danger."

He tried to conceal a deep- rooted sigh. The fear that was haunting him after returning from the police station, but that he could not disclose to them, now found expression. He told his daughter, "They might kill him. I must go there."

A phone call came from the terrorists the next morning. They had tortured Sonai and now they made him call his father. "Dad, rescue me. They'll kill me," he was crying on telephone. After that they took him away and one of them told Pramath, "We've abducted him and taken him to our camp at Pasaka in Bhutan. Save your son if you can."

Getting calls from Mumpi, Afroj and Boris arrived quickly at the house. "I'm coming with you. Last year I went to Thimpu to attend an international seminar on AIDS. There I chanced to meet a local youth. His name is Namgay. He told me that he had contact with the terrorists and he had gone to their camps several times. Before we go there I'll try to contact him," Afroj said.

Bhutan is one and a half hours' journey from Kolkata if a traveller wants to go by air. Druk Airways is the only airline which is allowed to fly into this country. Nestled on the Himalayas, Bhutan is a landlocked country between the Tibetan autonomous region of China in the North, and India in the South with formidable mountain terrains ranging from 100 meters to 7,500 meters in height. The aborigines of Bhutan, known as Monpa, are believed to have migrated from Tibet. The traditional name of the country is Drukyul, land of Drokpa.

Veiled under the sheet of mysteries, Bhutan has always enthralled the foreigners because her royal palace, monasteries, and gumphas always create curiosity in their minds. These gumphas were created by Sabdrung Ngawang Namgyel (literally at whose feet one submits), who was a Tibetan monk and founded the modern Bhutan state. He established himself as the country's supreme leader and ruled for 35 years. His successors ruled the country till 1907. He built dzongs as strong fortress and seats of the local governments. Besides, he built monasteries and religious institutions. He also set up the Drukpa Kargyupa school of Tantric Mahayana Buddhism in Bhutan.

Earlier the planes that would fly between Bhutan and India were 12-seater dorniers that lacked the system of pressure facility that could not allow the flights to move above the ceiling of the clouds. Naturally, the flight was very risky during turbulent weather because the planes would jerk recklessly that would obviously create panic among the fliers.

When the weather was not sunny, flights were often cancelled. Those who had had the experience of visiting India during those early days could recount pretty well how flights were cancelled at the last moment for inclement weather and how they had to extend their stay in the city hotels.

Besides, there were only three flights that would operate between Kolkata and Bhutan and the flights were without attendants and the passengers had to serve themselves food and beverage.

But now the situation is quite different. After the introduction of the airbus, flight between Kolkata and Bhutan remains operational five days in a week.

According to a security report, Bhutan's greatest security threat came from the terrorists of India's north-east states, who entered this country illegally and set up camps in the dense forests. The militants of the United Liberation Front of Assam (ULFA), the National Democratic Front of Bodoland (NDFB), and the Kamtapur Liberation Organization (KLO) were operating against Indian security forces from their bases in the southern, eastern, and central Bhutan.

In a 1993 issue of Bhutan's state-run weekly Kuensel it was reported that the KLO set up camps across the river Wangchu that was very close to Chukha. The presence of this terrorist group in close proximity to the hydro-power project was a major concern for the government of Bhutan.

According to another report, there were 19 to 20 camps of Indian insurgent groups inside Bhutan. The ULFA had eight camps inside the country with a total of 1,560 cadres. The NDFB had 740 cadres spread over eight camps. Finally, the KLO had 430 of its rebels in three or four camps inside Bhutan.

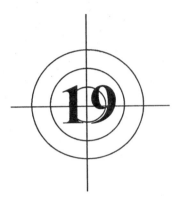

When the Druk Airbus touched the ground at Paro Airport, they saw they were surrounded by a chain of mountains. Mt. Chomolhari, which stands at the northern end of the Paro Valley, is the source of glacial water that flows through the deep gorges and after reaching the valley forms Pa Chu(the Paro River) that gives the most fertile land to Bhutan and this valley is the bowl of famous red rice of this country that is cultivated on the terraced fields of the valley.

They took a taxi from the airport. A narrow metallic road wound its way through the hills. As the car was approaching Thimpu, the road became wider. They were passing through a place where the hill was extremely bare and craggy. Far below, the river Thimpu was rumbling pleasantly. The driver told them, "There is a natural conch on this hill. Your journey will be successful if you can spot it at a glance." It was Pramath, who first noticed a large brown rock which was shaped like a conch on the hill.

They soon reached a place where they saw a large gate. On its top was written "Welcome to Thimpu". Next, the car was moving downward. They saw a large plush green valley dotted with beautiful houses whose roofs were pagoda shaped. The car was racing on a flyover that soon branched into several directions. The driver steered the car left and quickly drove to the centre of the city. They passed the oil station further to the heart of the city. The driver stopped the car outside a building.

They read the name of the road on a roadside signboard: it was Namzim Lam (in Bhutanese lam means road.). The driver advised them, "Look, this is the AV hotel. The Indian tourists put up here."

They paid the driver and walked towards the hotel. The ground floor was occupied with various shops. They asked one shop owner about the hotel. He pointed to a dark narrow staircase and said, "It's on the first floor."

Two young female receptionists were standing behind a counter in a large hall. Many people were sitting at the tables while consuming food and wine.

"We need a room," Afroj said, but all the rooms were booked. One receptionist informed them about another hotel. When they reached there, they realised that it was also completely booked. The hotelier advised them that just opposite this hotel there was another hotel and they should try there.

Pramath waited there while Afroj went to the new hotel. Pramath saw a group of Tamil-speaking tourists in the dining room. From their appearance he guessed they were village folk. The hotelier told him, "Very problem, sir, with these tourists. They can speak neither Hindi, nor Bhutanese."

In the meantime Afroj came back and informed him that one double bedroom was available in that hotel. Without delay, they set out for the hotel.

The signboard on the front of the hotel read "Rambsell". The ground floor of the hotel was below the level of the flyover. Walking across a concrete slab that connected the hotel to the outside road, they reached the first floor. The staircase led them to the second floor where there was a large swing door which led them into a spacious hall where one could see a large semi-circular desk. Bright-coloured heavy curtains were hanging from the windows. At the farthest nook of the hall, some sofa sets were arranged in front of a television set. Two young women were watching the television.

Those girls waddled towards the counter to welcome them. The aged one brought out the hotel register. They wrote their names and addresses. Then the younger lass walked them to a room. The interior of the room pleased them. The floor of the room was carpeted in azure blue. Though there was only one window, it was large and facing the south. When the girl pushed the curtain aside, a hill covered with snow appeared in the view. At one corner a television set was placed on a table. A large mahogany wardrobe was kept against one wall. In the middle of the room, there was a sofa and a table the top of which was made of some heavy glass.

After lunch Afroj telephoned Namgay and told him that he wanted to meet him. Namgay told him the address of a bar which was located in a very narrow lane far away from the hotel. The street was dark and some youths were playing cards under the balcony of the building. He stopped there to read the signboard. Then he pushed the glass door gently to enter.

A middle-aged bartender was standing behind the counter. Afroj asked him, "Where is Namgay? I want to meet him." The man told him to wait.

Afroj looked around. He saw that many men were drinking and in one corner of the room some people were smoking ganja. Few minutes later the bartender came back and told him to go to a cubicle at the farthest corner of the hall. Afroj saw that Namgay was drinking some wine, sitting alone. When Afroj entered the place, Namgay looked up and offered him a seat. After exchanging greetings, Afroj ordered a drink for himself. Then Afroj began to explain the purpose of his visit.

"You're entering into a lion's den. Any time your life can be terminated," Namgay warned him.

"We have no other choice," Afroj replied.

Next day they set out on their mission. Namgay told them that at first they would go to Phuentsholing, and then to Pasaka, where the terrorists had imprisoned Sonai. He advised them to purchase jack boots for protection against leeches in the forest, two sleeping bags and a high power torch. He would get a folding tent. From Phuentsholing they would buy dry food. Early in the morning, they left for Phuentsholing. They looked at the valley for the last time. Though they stayed a single night, they fell in love with this serene city.

A white fog enveloped the sleepy valley in the early morning. They were moving from the north to the south. As they were journeying down, the nature of forest on the hills was changing rapidly. So far they had seen dense pine forest, but when they were nearing Chukha, the hydel power project that was built with the technical know-how of India, they saw other trees that they could find in the plains. On the slopes they saw potatoes and sprouts and they also found oranges.

At Gedu they halted for a brief time for breakfast. When they were near to Phuentsholing they saw the road was partially blocked. Some boulders fell on the road from the hill. Two loaders were pushing those boulders towards the edge of the road. It took almost an hour to clear the road.

Due to this they couldn't reach Phuentsholing before 2.30 PM. After such a long journey they were hungry. Namgay took them to a hotel opposite the immigration office.

This small border town between India and Bhutan is vibrant with assimilation of cultures, dresses, food, customs, and languages of these two neighbouring countries. Lively river the Torsha flows few miles away from the town. All the twenty districts of Bhutan are connected by roads. The road winds north, over the southern foothills, through the lush woodland valleys and the north-south ridges of the inner Himalayas. Deep forests cover the mountains on both sides.

After lunch Namgay brought out a sticker from his bag with the words 'Tala Hydel Project' written on it and pasted it on the car's wind screen. Beside it he pasted his passport size photo with the attested signature of the Superintendent of Police. "Without it the police will not allow us to go to Pasaka. This is just to hoodwink them," he winked at Afroj and Pramath.

A short person, Namgay was dressed in a long rob tied at his waist, a little leather cap, and a pair of sports shoes.

Namgay was right because when they were heading towards Pasaka, they had to cross an old bridge where they saw a police checkpoint. Two policemen were checking the vehicles, but they did not bother to look at their car. Namgay waved at those policemen who smiled and waved in return.

Down below the road, they saw a river whose bed was dry. It was the river Torsha. Namgay pointed his finger at the left bank of the Torsha and said, "Look at the plains. Those places belong to India - most of them are tea gardens. Where the plains end and the highland starts, that is the border between India and Bhutan. This is the duars forest."

Then he pointed to a hill and said, "The terrorists have encamped on that hill."

Now, they were going downwards. On the way they noticed few factories - a ferro alloy factory, one brewery, and a soft drink bottling unit. They went past the beer unit and stopped in front of a makeshift stall. Some labourers were drinking country beer. Two women were serving them. Few minutes later a man appeared there holding a dead duck in one hand. It seemed that Namgay was waiting for that man.

Namgay asked him, "Where will you go?" He pointed to the hill. Namgay told him to sit in the car. He opened the door opposite his seat to let him in. The man was tipsy. His breath had the stench of some strong local liquor. Namgay asked him if he had seen some terrorists on the hill. He nodded his head. When Namgay told him to show the place, he informed him that the terrorists lived in a glade on the other side of the hill.

At one place the man told Namgay to stop the car. He told Namgay to get down from the car. He showed Namgay a trail on the hill almost shaded with trees and then departed. Namgay told Afroj what that man had shown. They looked at the trail that went steeply upward, winding its way through the trees and shrubs and finally, it was lost in the dense depth of the forest.

With crouching bent-knee steps, Namgay walked up the trail that led him into the forest. The others followed him with pounding heartbeats. The forest welcomed them with an ominous foreboding. So dense was the forest that even the sunrays didn't dare peep inside. The vast area was abandoned to the reign of vegetation - gigantic trees like teak, sal, chikrasi stood like guards from time immemorial; and fierce animals like bison, rhinos, leopards roamed freely in the jungle.

Duars which is divided into two parts- south duars and north duars- has had the presence of a range of hills that rose majestically northwards into Bhutan. The south duars, which is at the foot of these hills, is endowed with fertile soil, heavy green grass, and partly dense jungle. But the north duars, which is inside Bhutan, is steep, sometimes bare, craggy and extremely wayward. From a distance it seemed to Pramath that mauve hills stood majestically over the velvet green plains but coming close he observed that those hills were dark green as covered with the dense forest. Namgay informed them that the forests were the abode of many birds that would fill the forests with beautiful melodies. As they were descending southwards, the terrain was almost flat and covered with giant trees festooned with orchids. The terrains were crisscrossed with some great rivers like the Teesta and the Torsha and innumerable seasonal rivulets and springs whose dry pebbled beds enhanced the grandiosity of the vast virgin wilderness.

The forest looked like a tricky labyrinth, playing chiaroscuro with them as they dared to intrude into its domain. The very odor of the jungle was close to death - the rotten vegetation, the mass of fungi, the extraordinary height of the trees just confounded them. They were stumbling, at every footstep, on the herbs lying innocently on the trail. After two hours of trekking the trail met a small glade slopping down towards a stream whose bed was almost dry in winter. A slim course of water was flowing on its bed. Some goats were eating shrubs that cropped up inside the crevices of the rocks. Namgay remarked that the stream would become tumultuous during the rainy season. Small white pebbles were lying on the beds like silver lumps.

They followed the course of the small stream

meandering southwards. After another two hours they arrived at a ridge. They began to mount it; but it was so steep that they could manage only about few paces before they sat down and took rest. Loose stones were scattered away from under their feet. Even the most dangerous terrorist would panic if he looked at Pramath's hawk-nose, gaunt cheek bones covered with long unshaven silvery white whiskers, clenched lips, and the eyes which were gleaming like burning coal.

His habitual calm had deserted him. He was looking like a ferocious tiger that did not fear even the toughest foes. After a while, the thick scent of dead corpses reached their nostrils. They came across few dead men standing in different postures. Among them was the corpse of a thickset man whose cheeks and jaws were shattered and black-red pulp of flesh flowed out. Another corpse was of a youth whose eyes were gripped with a deadly horror and his mouth was twisted in utmost pain as if he was attempting to suck air, as his throat was slashed with a sharp dagger. The third one was wearing a soldier's uniform and his right hand gripped the butt of a revolver, dangling from his waist. His skull was destroyed with a bomb and the eyes were forked out.

Afroj started sobbing, looking at the corpse. Hurriedly, Pramath took him away from the spot.

Before daylight passed, they were able to reach the top of the ridge. The moon was washing the top with her white light and a cold wind was blowing down from the distant Himalayan peaks. The owls were hooting from the top of the trees ringing out an ominous tune over the hill. Afroj tried to light up some fire with some dry twigs after they put up the tent to pass the night, but Pramath promptly put out the fire. "Our hosts live at the foot of this ridge. Anytime they can spray us with bullets," he warned them. None could sleep that night; they were shivering in cold though they had put on sweaters, leather jackets, gloves and caps.

When dawn descended over the ridge, a grey flat glade appeared before them. Pramath adjusted his binoculars to watch the glade. At first he could see only some hazy shapes carved out of the jungle which looked like signs of human activity; but when sheets of fog disappeared, he saw some scary looking muscled men were standing and some lethal weapons were dangling from their waists.

When the day grew a bit older they descended from the ridge and walked towards the camp. The guards ran towards them, but when they saw Namgay they halted because they did not want to get into trouble with the local people. Namgay told them that he brought Pramath and Afroj to meet the commander.

"Who are these guys? Why have they come here?" the commander asked.

"They have come for a boy. This man is the father of the boy," Namgay replied.

"What is the name of his son?"

"Sonai."

The commander's face was knotted with anger. He shouted scornfully, "He is a traitor. We will kill him."

"I request you to know the fact. That's why I've brought them here. He is an innocent guy who has been trapped," Namgay appealed.

But the commander was not convinced.

"I know everything. Our men were following him from Kolkata. He was told to hand over two revolvers and the bullets to us; but he did not do it; rather he tried to flee. He is a traitor; so we'll kill him. Since you have dared to come here, you will also be our prisoners. Tomorrow we'll decide what to do with you," He told them.

21

They were taken into the tent where Sonai was
kept imprisoned. Faint black smoke was spiraling
upward from a lantern. In the half-light, Sonai was
sitting like a ghost. He was sitting with both hands
tied behind him. A short brown wooden pole was
driven into the ground at the centre of the tent and he
was tied to it with both hands tied behind him and
two legs fettered with iron chains. A steel collar was
strapped round his neck so deftly that, though it was
not strangling him, but immobilizing any movement
of his head and neck; and as a result he had to sit
straight. His face was distorted with immense pain
and fear.

A nail that jutted out from the collar by the mechanism of a screw touched his Adam's apple; and any forward movement of his head would obviously let the nail pierce his throat.

Pramath could not control his tears when he saw Sonai in that condition.

Few minutes later a guard came there to take Pramath into the commander's tent. "Are you an army officer?" asked the commander. His look was loaded with hatred.

"Yes," Pramath answered boldly.

"Every Indian soldier is our enemy." The commander ordered the guards to take Pramath into the torture chamber.

Pramath was thrust on a chair and his hands and legs were strapped. A scary-looking gigantic terrorist came forward with two electrodes. He touched them on Pramath"s hands, legs and genital parts. Pramath was crying out in mortal pain as the current was passing through his body. The silence of the forest was shattered by his screams. They tortured him till midnight and then dragged his body to the tent where others were kept.

They thought that after such inhuman torture Pramath would be finished; but they were wrong; he was specially trained to endure extreme physical torture in the army. He was remembering those bloody days in the Kargil War when he and his colleagues were climbing the rugged mountains at the Batalic sector and fighting the enemies with knives.

No telescopic rifles, no cannon, nothing. Simple hand-to-hand fight with knives where either one kills or is killed - the primitive rule of nature.

At midnight a man entered the tent. Sonai saw that the visitor was none other than Robin, the youth whom he had met in the bus.

"Do you recognize me? Now, you know why I sat beside you. We followed you. The revolvers and the bullets were scheduled to reach our hand. Unfortunately, our next team was late in reaching the Blue Diamond. When they visited your room you had already escaped. You put up in a new hotel. They appeared there and the rest you know. But they committed a mistake. They could not realize that you had left the boxes in the Blue Diamond itself. However, those who made the mistake received punishment. Their bodies were thrown from the hilltop. In our work there is no mercy for such mistakes," Robin said.

"Why have you come here now? To tell me all these shit!" Sonai said sarcastically.

"I've come to inform you that they have decided to kill you in the morning. But I see that you're not afraid," Robin informed.

"My heart assures me that we'll not be killed, because it is not in our destiny. Let me tell you a story. In the southern part of India there was a small kingdom named Vijaynagar. The people would live a very peaceful life under the good governance of a noble king. But that peace was destroyed by a band of brigands who ushered in a reign of terror. Murder, rape and robbery became every day's event. When the king heard the plight of his subjects, he became angry and ordered his lieutenant to arrest those dacoits. He warned him that he would behead him if he could not arrest the dacoits. The lieutenant went into the jungle to arrest the dacoits but he could not find them. Had he come back empty-handed the king would kill him. At that time he saw a woodcutter in the forest. An evil thought came in the lieutenant's mind. He ordered his guards to arrest that woodcutter. They brought the woodcutter in front of him. He told the poor man, 'How dare you cut trees in this forest? Don't you know that it is king's favourite forest? You're a dacoit; so we'll impale you.' The man fell to his knees and implored the wicked lieutenant to forgive him. But as usual no mercy was shown to the man. He was fettered in irons to exhibit how dangerous dacoit he was. The lieutenant was riding on a horse with a sword whose blade was glistening in sunrays. People gathered on either side of the road to see the dacoit. The news soon reached the king that the dacoit leader was captured. He awarded the lieutenant a diamond ring.

The king had some spies who would roam around the kingdom to know if anybody was plotting against the king. Two days later, after the capture of the innocent woodcutter, a spy chanced to hear strange talks in an inn. He heard that some men were discussing how the lieutenant fooled the king by passing a woodcutter as a dacoit. The spy looked at those persons cautiously. He saw that they were the soldiers of the royal army. The spy reached the palace to inform the king. He saw that the guards had brought the woodcutter in the ground to impale him on a spear. Thousands of people thronged there to witness the impalement of the dacoit. But the woodcutter was laughing. The king asked him, 'Why are you laughing? Aren't you afraid?' 'I'm laughing at my destiny. I'm a simple woodcutter, but my destiny has framed me as a dacoit,' the poor man replied.

The spy told the guard that he wanted to meet the king because he had some important information to give the king. But the guard did not let him go to the king. The spy was insisting but the guard was determined that he would not allow the spy. Hearing some chaos at the entrance, the king ordered the other guards to bring in the man who was insisting on meeting him. They brought the spy before him. The king recognized him and asked, 'Why are you insisting on meeting me?' The spy made a long bow before the king and said, 'If you give me assurance, I can give you a piece of information.' The king said, 'You can tell me fearlessly.' Then the spy said, 'O king, this man is not a dacoit. He is a woodcutter. Your lieutenant has framed him as a dacoit leader.' The rest of this tale is easily understandable. The king released the woodcutter and ordered the guards to impale the lieutenant," Pramath told them the story that he heard from his grandma.

Robin remained silent for few seconds, and then said, "The woodcutter's destiny was kind to him, but I'm such a man whose destiny dragged him into abysmal pain. Let me tell you my story. I lived in a beautiful village with my parents. The village was surrounded by forests, hills and rivers. The people of that village were simple and honest. They were content with what nature gave them. One day some people came from a far away country. At first they lured us with money. Some of us handed them their land in lieu of money; but others didn't. Then those foreigners evicted us from our land. I fled into the forest. There I found that many people had already gathered and they were saying that they would fight against the foreigners. Someone from us said that some terrorists who would live in the forest would help us. I was very excited to know who those people were how they looked. Many years later, when I grew up, I understood that they were also people of our country.

We arrived at the centre of the forest where we saw that hundreds of people gathered. They were a restless lot. I was very disappointed when I saw that they were just like us. But they were wearing strange clothes and carrying long sticks. Later, I came to know that the clothing was military uniform and the sticks were guns. Suddenly, a man appeared before us. Someone whispered in my ears, 'He is the leader of these terrorists.' I noticed that the leader was flanked by dozens of guards. He stood before us and thundered, 'Comrades, we've gathered here for a noble cause. Our mission is to drive out the foreigners from our motherland. We have to shed blood; we have to embrace death; but we must not stop till we achieve our goal.

We underwent guerrilla training to learn how to combat the police and the army. We were divided into small groups and sent to training camps deep in the jungle. The rule of the camp was that there would be no sound and light at night. At dawn we had to get up from beds and do jogging, perform various physical exercises, and practice crawling on the grounds with heavy bags on the back. We learnt to copy bird calls - different birds like peacocks, doves, cuckoos. After lunch we would take some rest and then again we would undergo drills and exercise for two hours. Three months passed. Then we were given training of shooting from rifles and revolvers and combating with knives. Finally, we were given training of the use of the explosives like RDX. When I would return to my tent I could not stand up straight and would slouch. I would want to cry, but could not - the leader's voice would come as resurgence in my ears.

We could not ask any personal questions about the fellow men. The trainer would strictly keep an eye on us. One day I was told to go to a town along with two terrorists. It was a beautiful town with old houses, schools, playgrounds and hospitals. We were waiting in front of a large store. A car was parked there. My companions ordered me to put a box in the bonnet of the car. When I was returning, I saw a beautiful girl was running towards the car with her parents. As soon as her father started the engine a huge explosion took place, and the car was lifted into the air like a fireball. My companions grabbed my hands and ran towards the forest. I was perplexed but I was sure that the box caused the explosion. When I grew older, I came to know that it was a bomb. But I could not forget the face of that girl - it was so innocent and cute. I realised that I was trapped by some butchers. Since then I've lived with pain and anguish. But I've not had the courage to desert them. Everyday I have to witness the carnage of innocent people. Nowadays I hate myself."

"I can feel your pain. You were misguided at an early age but there is still time to change your way of life," Pramath assured him.

"But how? I'm so scared," Robin asked.

"That's because you've always listened to your mind that has always instigated you to avenge yourself on the wrongdoers, but had you listened to your heart's voice you could understand that revenge was not the solution for rectifying wrong. Only love and respect for others can bring peace and only then one community can live in harmony with others. There are so many people who mourn that their life is fraught with misfortunes, and they are buffeted by others, but if they think from other side they will find that such bad things are gateway to new happenings in life," Pramath replied.

"I fell in love with a woman of our gang. We got married and a baby was born. Six months ago my wife was killed by the police. I request you to take my son with you because I don't want him to be a killer. Tomorrow, when they will find that you are not in the cell and my son is also gone, they will understand that I have done it. They will kill me, but I don't care. My life is so rotten that I would prefer to die," Robin said.

Before dawn he set them free and said, "There is a river half-mile away from this place. After crossing it, you'll find a village. Go there. They will help you."

They crawled towards the jungle. This time they were going to the opposite direction. Robin gave Pramath a revolver with a silencer and said, "There will be two guards sitting on a tree at the start of the jungle. You've to kill them."

Those guards were dozing. With accurate aim Pramath killed both of them. The bodies tumbled down but before the bodies touched the ground, Afroj and Namgay caught them and hid them behind the thick foliage.

They were fleeing southwards. In the dark that enveloped them, they were stumbling at each footstep but their sheer survival instinct compelled them to move on. The hill was extremely wayward and steep. They had to climb down very cautiously because any slight mistake would result in the fall down the rocky hill. But the dense forest came to their support at that time because they could move with the support of the branches of the trees, but the presence of the boy made the trek arduous.

Namgay was leading the team. Pramath put the boy on his shoulder. At five in the morning they could hear the rippling sound of water. Namgay cried out, "We've reached the river." It was meandering down leaping on the white boulders. They began to follow the river course. The bed of the river was shallow, but they were walking along the bank. They feared that the child might cry for his father, but he remained silent throughout the journey!

Pramath asked him several times, Are you okay? Are you tired? But each time the boy replied that he was all right. At seven in the morning they reached the foot of the hill. There they saw a small sleepy village. The doors were closed from within. They knocked on a door. After some time a man came out with sleepy eyes. He was surprised to see them. When they told him how they had run away from the terrorist camp, the man was bewildered. His drowsiness vanished. He called in his wife. She took them inside the hut and told them that the terrorists had contacts even in the village. If they knew that they had escaped from their camp, they would inform the terrorists who would attack the village and take them away again. They advised them to leave the place as soon as possible.

They escorted them to Hasimara and helped them board a bus that was going to Siliguri. The boy was in Afroj's lap. Unfortunately, when they were halfway from Siliguri, one of the rear tyres punctured. Luckily, a mechanic was available in a nearby dhaba. While the driver and the mechanic were changing the tyre, Pramath was continuously looking at his wristwatch. Tension was mounting on everyone. Anytime those terrorists could come to kill them.

At last the mechanic changed the tyre and by the evening they reached Siliguri. Although the bus was supposed to go ahead to Kolkata, the driver asked them to board another bus as the driver found some mechanical fault in the engine of the bus. The driver arranged a new bus but an hour was wasted in this process. When the bus was about to start, Pramath embraced Namgay and said, "I'm indebted to you, my friend." Namgay became emotional and was crying.

It was seven o'clock at night when the bus started running. They waved to Namgay, who was waiting there till the bus was in sight. Then Afroj talked to Mumpi by mobile phone and assured her that they were safe and would reach Bibeknagar the next day. Pramath and Afroj discussed and at last decided that the child should be sent to the orphanage where Pramath was attached.

The day Pramath set out for Bhutan, Sonali and Boris went to Boris's father-in-law's house. When they arrived there, they saw that the floors were decorated with "alpanas". She told Boris, "Sure, ma has done it in honor of her son-in-law." Mitali, Amal's mother-in-law was in the kitchen. Hearing their voice, she came out. He bent down to touch her feet. Sonali asked her mom, "Where is dad?"

"In the bedroom, as usual," replied Mitali.

Sonali's dad, Niraud Mukherjee, was a retired employee of Indian Railways. After superannuation, he would spend time by reading newspapers and watching serials on television. He was a very funny person who would call himself "genetically lazy".

In the evening, Boris went to the roof. The

daylight was quickly passing out. Some thrushes were flying around, creating a circle right in the middle of the sky. Stars were coming out from the belly of the sky. A gentle breeze was playing about the leaves of the tall trees that were standing around the house.

Some women from the neighborhood visited the house to see the British son-in-law. Though Mitali and Niraud expected and Sonali requested Boris, he convinced them that they must return home because Pramath had requested Boris to look after his family. After returning home, Sonali was taking a rest in bedroom and Boris was chatting with her sitting at the edge of the bed; suddenly, they heard that someone was knocking at the door frantically. When Boris opened the door, he saw Mumpi was standing there, panting violently. She told him, "I was returning from the computer centre. Some youths followed me from the gate of the auditorium."

Then Boris escorted her to the house. Pratima was frightened when she heard it.

Pratima and Mumpi woke up very early in the morning to decorate the whole house as if it was a festive day. Pratima was preparing her son's favourite dishes while Mumpi was helping her. Innumerable times they ran to the front door to see if Sonai had come. At last a car stopped outside the house and Sonai stepped out from the car. After reaching Kolkata by bus, they hired the car.

After so many days' waiting Pratima got back her son; naturally, she was crying in joy. Everyone in the house became emotional and was sobbing. It was a new sunrise for the whole family after the long hours of darkness.

After rescuing Sonai from the terrorists' den, one day Pramath went to the muhallah where Afjal would live. A neighbour showed him Afjal's house - a dilapidated one-storied building. Pramath knocked at the door. A youth came out. Pramath introduced himself.

The youth took him into the house. They entered a dark room. It was Afjal's bedroom. The youth switched on the lamp. Pramath asked him about Afjal. The youth said, "Afjal was an orphan who would live in an orphanage. One day the in-charge of the orphanage beat him after a staff member complained that Afjal had stolen cash from his room. After that incident Afjal fled away from the orphanage. Gradually, he engaged himself in antisocial activities."

Pramath's memory went into flashback. Few years ago...a fifteen-year-old boy whom Boris rescued from platform and he gave shelter in the orphanage stole cash from a staff member's room... Now everything became clear to him. That boy was none other than Afjal. Pramath could not help asking that youth, "Did he really steal that money?"

"No," answered that youth, "He told me that some other boy stole the money and kept it in his box."

Relatives and neighbours who were avoiding Pramath's family now crowded in his house to hear how he freed Sonai from the grip of the terrorists. But the joy of Sonai's homecoming was short-lived as the police arrested him next day after his arrival at home and sent him to the interrogation chamber where Bikramjeet was waiting for him. Initially, Bikramjeet thought that he had to apply third degree method to wrest out information from Sonai, but his family background impressed Bikramjeet. He began to believe that Sonai could not be involved in the arms deal, as he was the son of an honest man like Pramath. Later, when Bikramjeet visited Anil Sen, he asked Bikramjeet, "Has the bastard confessed anything?"

Bikramjeet narrated everything that Sonai had told him and at last commented, "Sir, I feel he is speaking the truth."

"Pooh! I don't believe it."

"Sir, I think he is speaking the truth. We should release him," repeated Bikramjeet.

"Are you crazy? Can't you realise what will happen? Leaders will kick our ass," Anil cried in panic.

"But sir, should we convict an innocent person?" Bikramjeet still appealed.

"How can you be so confirmed that he is innocent? All the evidence is against him. Besides, don't forget that our boss won't spare us if we fail to put someone on the gallows," Anil revealed the fact.

When the police took Sonai in their custody, Pratima locked herself in a room. Everyone- Boris, Mumpi, Afroj- was extremely sad. Afroj knelt down before Pramath and holding both his hands said, "Uncle, please do something."

"What can I do?" Pramath asked helplessly.

"At present we've to appoint a lawyer," Afroj suggested.

"But I don't know any lawyer," Pramath said.

"Dad, my friend, Avijit Basu, has a brother-in-law who is a lawyer. We can contact him," Mumpi suggested. Without wasting any time, she telephoned Avijit. Fortunately, he was at home at that time. He told Pramath, "Don't worry. My brother-in-law, Ranajoy Sen, is an ace lawyer. He has been practicing for many years. We will go to his chamber in the evening."

In the evening, when they reached Ranajoy's chamber they saw that the place was crowded with clients. Craning his neck from behind the crowd Avijit said loudly, "Hi, boss! How are you? I need to talk to you."

A smile flashed across Ranajoy's face when he saw Avijit. "Wait a second," he said. He was busy talking to some client. After the client departed, he beckoned them to come. Pramath followed Avijit. Having heard Pramath's misfortune, he commented, "The circumstantial evidence is against your son. So I can't give you any hope. All I can say is that we have to work very hard. First of all, we have to appear before the court and seek his bail."

Sonai escaped from his home on the 3rd of November and after eleven days the police could arrest him. They already framed a case against Salem. This time they tagged Sonai to this case. Sonai's bail plea was rejected by the judge and he was remanded into the police custody for a week.

Ranajoy visited him in the police custody. Sonai told him everything - from the very first day when Mumpi saw him with Afjal to his capture by the terrorists. Then he requested Ranajoy, "Please, sir. Don't reveal to my parents what I've told you. They won't be able to bear the shock. I've told them that I went to Siliguri with my friends."

"All right. I won't disclose it to them. But you've to give me the names of your most trusted friends who will say before the court that they had planned to go to Siliguri with you, but at the last moment they had to cancel their program due to some personal problems."

Later, when Pramath visited him in his chamber, he said, "The receptionist of the hotel Sunrise will be a vital eyewitness before the court. You have to go to Siliguri."

"Shall he comply with my requests?" Pramath asked sceptically.

"No. he will not. We have to depend on some private detective agency. A friend of mine who is a retired police officer runs such an agency. I'll request him to help you. You'll contact me two days later."

Two days later when Pramath telephoned Ranajoy, he said, "I was just waiting for your phone call. I told you that a friend of mine is a police officer. He has agreed to go with you. Don't worry. He will manage everything. But you have to leave for Siliguri today because we have only three days left before the hearing starts."

Ranajoy's friend, Preetam Paul, was a retired

police officer. He told Pramath, "We will stay at the hotel Sunrise." Sonai told them that the receptionist's name was Santanu Roy. Preetam told a boy, "We are coming from Santanu's neighbourhood. He told us that he works in this hotel."

The boy told them, "He will come at 5 p.m."

In the afternoon Preetam went to the reception desk to meet Santanu. He was a young man. Preetam told him, "My nephew had come to Siliguri to participate in the All Bengal Tennis Tournament. He told me that he had stayed in this hotel."

"What's the name of your nephew?" Santanu asked.

"Sonai."

Hearing the name, Santanu was startled.

"Sorry. He did not stay here," he promptly answered.

Preetam understood that Santanu was telling a blatant lie. He showed Santanu a passport size photograph of Sonai and said, "Look at the photo. I think that it will help you refresh your memory." But Santanu denied seeing Sonai.

Then Preetam told him, "I'm coming from the intelligence department. I've come to know that Sonai Biswas was kidnapped from your hotel. Two guys did it and you helped them."

Santanu panicked and broke down in tears. "Believe me, sir. I do not know anything. At gunpoint they forced me to go into his room," he told Preetam.

"You call in at my room with the hotel register

within ten minutes," Preetam ordered him. Santanu appeared before him within five minutes.

Preetam told him to open the register where Sonai had written his name and address, but that particular page was missing. Preetam asked him, "Why have you done it, rascal?" Santanu remained silent.

Preetam guessed that such an offence might have been committed; therefore, he placed a tape recorder under the sofa before Santanu came in the room. Now, he ordered Santanu to recount what happened on that particular day. Santanu could not imagine that every word of his statement was being recorded.

Throughout the process Pramath was a silent spectator. Now, he stood up and putting his hands on Santanu's shoulders, spoke, "I bless you from my heart. You don't know what goodness you have done to my family. My only son who was kidnapped by some terrorists is in police custody. The police believe that he is involved with the terrorists. Your statement will prove that he is not involved with them."

"Are you not cops?" Santanu was highly confused.

"I'm an ex-army officer. My friend is a retired police officer and is very well known at the top level of the police department," Pramath replied.

"Since the life of an innocent person depends on you, I hope that you won't backtrack on your statement," Preetam said sternly.

After seven days' remand in the police custody
Sonai was produced before the court for trial. The
courtyard and the courtroom were brimming with
the curiosity of the media as well as the common
men. No sooner had Sonai got down from the police
van than some men began to jeer at him. Police put a
mask on his face and hurriedly took him into the
courtroom. When the trial began, the public
prosecutor began to apprise the judge how Sonai
worked for Salem, how Sonai brought two revolvers
into the hotel room of the Blue Diamond. As evidence
he produced the statement of Afjal, and two revolvers
and bullets that police seized from the Blue Diamond.
Then he produced the hotel register before the court
where Sonai wrote down his name and address.

After the public prosecutor finished his argument, Ranajoy began his defence argument. He asked the court, "Sir, have you ever heard of an instance where a person who supplies arms writes down his original name and address in the register book of a hotel? It's preposterous. The police have framed my client in a false case. They could not arrest my client from the Blue Diamond. In fact they could not arrest the real culprit and now to cover up their failure they are trying to put my client on the gallows."

The judge adjourned the case for that day and ordered both sides to present their witness before the court on 26th November.

Sonai was transferred from the police custody to the jail custody. He was kept with the hardcore criminals. His parents, sister, and Afroj visited him in the jail. He had grown a long beard and become very lean. His eyes sank deep inside the sockets; the facial structure underwent an awful change with protruding cheekbone and sagging jaw. The whole face was coated with a black pallor, and he was looking much older than his actual age. At first Pratima could not recognize him.

Then she cried out, "Oh, my God! What have they done to you?"

"Mama, please get me out of this hell. It is very stifling here. There are some murderers in my cell. They eat my food. They torture me. If I protest, they threaten to kill me," he said.

"Immediately complain to the jailor," she told Pramath.

"I've already done that. I have even bribed the guards. They promised me that such things won't happen in future." He answered helplessly.

When the visiting time was over, the guards told them to leave the place. Sonai took Mumpi aside, and muttered, "Sister, there is a girl named Puma. I met her few months ago. She lives at 49 Robertson Road. Please tell her to come here. I want to meet her." He gave Mumpi her number.

Mumpi called Puma once she reached home. But when she informed Puma that Sonai was in jail, she felt an uneasy silence on the other side.

"Hello, are you listening to me?" Mumpi asked.

"I've to go to Mumbai. It's urgent. I'll call you later," Puma said.

But never did she contact Mumpi. Or Sonai.

Five days later, when the court sat for the hearing, the police produced the receptionist, the boy and the commissionaire of the hotel Blue Diamond as their witnesses.

They told the court that Sonai stayed in the hotel and few hours later departed from the hotel. Then again, half an hour later after his departure, two men arrived at the hotel in search of him. The receptionist apprised the court how he discovered two revolvers and bullets from under the bed after the departure of those two people. The commissionaire of the hotel also confirmed that he had seen Sonai to come out of the hotel.

"My lord, they have given statements to the police

that the accused went outside the hotel immediately after checking into the hotel. Again, he did not take much time to check out. Then after his departure, two guys came to the hotel in search of him. So it was clear as daylight that the accused went to a telephone booth to contact his aides. Later, they came to the hotel to rescue him, but he had already left the hotel. The police could find only the black car which they used for the escape in abandoned condition in the forest," the public prosecutor told the judge.

Thereafter, Ranajoy began his cross-examination. He asked the hotel receptionist, "Did you find the revolvers and bullets after the exit of my client?"

"No," answered the receptionist.

"Point to be noted, my lord. The witness did not find those revolvers and bullets after the exit of my client which means that my client did not bring those revolvers and bullets into the hotel. Someone else brought them."

Then he asked the receptionist, "Did the police tell you that they came to the hotel because they had prior information that a terrorist was put up at the hotel?"

"No," replied the receptionist.

"Point to be noted, my lord. My learned friend told the court that my client had information that the police could raid the hotel any time, but the witness is telling us that they had no such information. In fact they arrived at the hotel only when the receptionist informed them. My friend has forgotten that words like "possibly", "probability" have no meaning in the eye of law. Law always demands concrete evidence. On the basis of my learned friend's arguments a fine fictitious story can be spun, but an innocent person cannot be convicted."

The court adjourned for that day.

Ranajoy met Sonai's friends, Dev and Kumar, in his chamber. "Your friend is in deep trouble. You will tell the court only what I tell you," he said.

They assured him, "Don't worry. We'll do everything to save our friend. We will tell the court only what you instruct us to tell."

When Ranajoy called them in the court as witnesses, they informed the court that they had planned to visit Siliguri and it was decided that Sonai would go ahead and book a room and they would join him later. Unfortunately, they had to cancel their trip because Dev's father was seriously ill and Kumar himself was not feeling well.

The next witness was the owner of the small shop outside the hotel Blue Diamond.

"What's your name?" Ranajoy asked him.

"Mahavir Singh."

"What do you do?"

"I have a small shop outside the hotel Blue Diamond."

"Look at the accused properly and tell the court if you have seen him."

"Yes."

"Tell the court when you saw him?"

"This man came to me on the 4th of November to ask about a hotel."

"Did you not ask him why he wanted the information?"

"Yes, I did."

"What did he answer?"

"He told me that the room service of the hotel Blue Diamond was very bad."

"Did you give him the address of another hotel?"

"I gave him the address of the hotel Sunrise."

"What did he do then?"

"He boarded an autorickshaw and went to the hotel Sunrise."

The public prosecutor decided to cross-examine Mahavir Singh.

"How do you know that the accused went to the hotel Sunrise?"

"I heard him when he called an autorickshaw."

"What! An autorickshaw? Tell the court in detail what happened after the accused came to you."

"He asked me how he could go to the Sunrise. I told him that he could go there by an autorickshaw. At that time an autorickshaw was coming down the road. He boarded it and asked the driver to take him to the hotel Sunrise."

"What was the distance between the autorickshaw and you?"

"It was almost 25 feet."

"What were you doing at that time?"

"I was busy arranging empty bottles in the crates."

"Point to be noted, my lord. The minimum distance between the stall and the auto rickshaw was 25 feet and the witness was busy at that time. So it was not possible for the witness to hear what the accused told the autorickshaw driver."

Ranajoy stood up to produce his next witness. "I want to produce such evidence that will prove that my client put up at the hotel Sunrise and from there he was abducted by the terrorists."

Then Ranajoy played the taped version of Santanu, the receptionist of the Sunrise. Everyone present in the courtroom could hear how two terrorists visited the hotel for Sonai, how they forced the hotel receptionist to take them to the room where Sonai put up and how they abducted him at gunpoint.

The judge wanted to know whose voice it was. Ranajoy informed him that it was the receptionist of the hotel Sunrise; but the public prosecutor argued that the recorded voice could not be accepted as a proof unless the person himself gave his witness before the court. The judge agreed with him and ordered Ranajoy to produce the receptionist before the court. Ranajoy begged the judge to grant him at least two days to produce Santanu. The judge granted his appeal.

That very day Pramath went to Siliguri. This time Mumpi accompanied him. Santanu was astonished when he saw.

"How are you, sir? Has your son been released?" he asked Pramath.

"I've come to you with a request. The court has ordered us to present you before the court so that you can tell the judge exactly what happened to Sonai."

"But how can I go? I can't take leave." Santanu was hesitant.

"Please, sir. The life of my brother depends on your deposition. Have mercy on us." Mumpi importuned him, holding his hands. Santanu looked at her dolorous eyes which were pleading for compassion. In his profession he met numerous women - cynics, puritans, finicky woman, coquette, and a lot more; but she was quite different.

"She is a gem. He who will marry her would be the luckiest guy in the world. She is not only beautiful, but has a great character," he thought to himself and made up his mind that he would go with them. He assured them that he would try to convince the manager so that he could get leave. She told him, "I hope that you'll not dishearten me."

"Oh, I can kill myself for those eyes!" he thought.

Santanu told a lie to the manager that he had received a phone call from his house that his mother was very ill and he must go home. The manager granted him a week's leave.

In the afternoon he knocked at the room where Mumpi and Pramath were staying. Only Mumpi was present in the room at that time. Pramath had gone to the local market. When Santanu gave the news, she gave him a grateful smile and said, "I knew that you would not disappoint me."

When Pramath heard that Santanu had agreed to come with them, he proposed that they should start immediately. Santanu agreed.

They were going to Bibeknagar by bus. Santanu and Pramath sat on a two-seater on the right side of the bus and Mumpi sat in the front, sharing a three-seater on the left side of the bus. At night whenever she woke up, she found that Santanu was looking at her.Next day they arrived at Bibeknagar at noon. After such a long bus journey, Santanu was very tired. He wanted to have a shower; so Mumpi showed him the bathroom and put a fresh set of towels and soap in his hand. When she was giving him those items, he lightly pressed her hand.

When he came out from the bathroom after having a shower, he saw that they were waiting for him at the dining table. Pramath told him, "I apologize for this simple fare. Since I was not at home my wife had to arrange everything." Pratima and Mumpi were serving Santanu. After lunch Pramath told him, "You must be very tired after this long journey. My guest room is ready. Have a sound sleep. We will talk in the evening."

The guest room was behind the main building. Gourav was not only a successful lawyer but he was a socialite and often guests would put up at his home. The guest room was specially built for that purpose. After Gourav's death it was never used and kept under lock and key. Santanu lit a cigarette and inhaled deeply. The lunch was a grand feast. He looked for an ashtray, but he could not find it in the room. He went to the window to shed the ash outside the room. He saw that Mumpi was feeding her pet dog. He stood there, watching her till the cigarette burnt his finger. Then he retired to bed and soon fell into a deep slumber.

He slept till evening. When he woke up, he saw that it was past six. After changing dress, he appeared in the drawing room. Pratima was watching some serial on television. She greeted him.

"Your husband and daughter don't seem to be at home," he said.

"He has gone to the lawyer's chamber. And Mumpi is on the roof," she answered.

"May I go to the roof?" he sought her permission.

"Of course."

The roof was bristling with the sound of the birds which were returning to their nests on the tall teak trees. The sky was neither black nor white. Some stars were twinkling in the sky. Mumpi was looking at the street. She was so engrossed in her own thoughts that she could not know when he came on the roof.

She was startled when he told her, "Hi! Your mom tells me that you're here."

She smiled.

"Your brother visited Siliguri alone! You should have accompanied him. Then such an accident mightn't have happened," he continued.

"No, it was decided that his two friends would accompany him. But later they cancelled their programme," she replied cautiously.

Santanu had been attracted to her since the time he saw her at the hotel. Now, when nobody was there on the roof, he tried to reveal his intention to her.

"The moment I saw you I knew that I can't live without you. I've come here only for your sake; otherwise I would have never agreed to be a witness," he told her.

Mumpi became alert to his intention. To change

the topic she asked him, "Have you got tea?" But he was not ready to slip the chance and dared to hold her hand which she quickly removed and briskly went downstairs.

Mumpi was suffering from guilt feelings after the abduction of Sonai. She could not forgive herself for his escape from home. She believed that she was responsible for his plight. She would constantly blame herself for the pain and affliction that her brother was passing through. When Ranajoy told them, that Santanu was the only person whose witness could save Sonai, she decided to go the whole hog to save Sonai; even she was ready to satisfy Santanu's lust for the sake of her brother.

Santanu waited few minutes after Mumpi went down. Then he came down slowly and entered the drawing room. He was an ace player in this game. He knew very well that she was entrapped so badly that it was impossible for her to free herself from his net.

Entering the drawing room, he saw that a visitor had arrived there. Mumpi took the visitor into her room and few moments later she went out with that visitor. Before departing, she came to the drawing room to say goodbye. Santanu perceived from her body language that she had accepted his proposal. After their exit, he asked Pratima, "Who is this gentleman?"

"Afroj! He went to the terrorists' den," she answered.

"Where have they gone now?" Santanu expressed

his ugly curiosity.

"To a computer centre where she works,"
Perhaps he would ask more questions, but she did
not like his questioning. She excused herself and went
to the kitchen.

Mumpi returned home at half past nine. Santanu
was watching a show on the television in the drawing
room, but actually he was waiting for her. He noticed
that she went to the roof instead of coming to the
drawing room. He followed her and reached the roof.
There he embraced her.

"Please, you're hurting me," she cried, but
tightening his hold on her soft body, he said, "I won't
leave you unless you give me my answer."

"The day after tomorrow you'll appear in court to
save my brother. After that I'll go to your room at
night, but after this incident you'll not meet me again;
never."

After saying this, she left the place hurriedly.

At night Pramath informed Santanu, "Tomorrow
I'll take you to my advocate. He'll tell you how to
answer before the judge."

Ranajoy tutored Santanu how to tell the court
who kidnapped Sonai from the hotel. Next day
Santanu appeared in court to give his witness. At
half past two he was summoned before the court.

Ranajoy started first.

"What is your name?"

"Santanu Roy."

"What do you do?"

"I'm a receptionist of the hotel Sunrise."

"Have you ever seen the accused?"

"Yes."

"Where have you seen him?"

"On 4th November he came to the hotel and sought a room."

"Did you give him a room?"

"Yes."

"What did he do then?"

"He went to his room."

"What time it was?"

"It was around one o'clock."

"What happened thereafter?"

"At quarter to two, two men came to the reception desk. They told me, 'We know that the son of a rich person of Kolkata has put up in your hotel. In fact, he has checked in few moments ago. Give us his room number.' At first I denied them the information. Then they aimed a revolver at me and ordered me to lead them to the room where this person put up. They forced me to tell this man to open the door and when he opened the door, they pounced upon him and then led him to a black car and within minutes whisked him away. The whole operation took place very quickly."

Then the public prosecutor began to question Santanu.

"Why did you not inform the police when you saw that two men kidnapped one of your guests?" he asked.

"I was very scared in case they came to know that I went to the police."

"Then why are you telling it now?"

"I am equally scared, but this man (pointing at Pramath) came to me and pleaded that the life of his son is depending on my witness. This prompted me to change my earlier decision. I thought that it was my duty to save the life of an innocent person."

"My lord, is it believable that a man who did not dare inform the police about the abduction of one of his guests suddenly became so brave that now he has appeared before the court to record his witness? There must be some other story behind it. We have no need to take this statement into account because the police have already placed sufficient evidence before this court that is enough to convict the accused. First of all, there is the deathbed confession of Afjal. Secondly, those two revolvers and bullets which the police seized from the hotel room are strong evidence. Thirdly, there is the hotel Blue Diamond's register, where the accused put down his name and address. Last but not the least, the receptionist of the hotel Blue Diamond has identified the accused. So there can't be any element of doubt that the accused has links with the terrorists," the public prosecutor told the court.

Ranajoy stood up again to defend Sonai. "My lord, the police have become so shameless that nowadays they don't hesitate to frame innocent people as terrorists. From the deposition given by Dev, Kumar and Santanu, it is as clear as broad daylight that my client is in no way associated with the terrorists. Now, it is an established fact that Sonai, Dev, and Kumar wanted to visit Siliguri, but Dev and Kumar could not go due to their personal problems. Unfortunately, Sonai had to go alone and he was abducted from the hotel Sunrise."

Outside the court, Ranajoy told Pramath, "I'm pretty sure the judge will acquit Sonai."

On the day of the final verdict of the court, everyone was filled with tension as the judge was preparing himself to give his final judgement. Pramath and Pratima, Mumpi and Afroj, Boris and Sonali - everyone- came to the courtroom to hear the final verdict of the judge. Press reporters, cameramen and common people, who were aware of the case through newspaper reports and coverage on the news channels, had also gathered there.

The judge took his seat. There was absolute silence when he began to read his verdict. Sonai was pretty sure he was going to be released.

"Having heard the arguments of the defence counsel and taking into view the evidence that the police department could place before the court......I do hereby pronounce that Mr. Sonai Biswas is guilty."

Pramath could not believe his ears. Pratima could not absorb the trauma and fainted in the courtroom. She was carried outside the courtroom and laid on a bench. Sonai was crying bitterly like a child.

Their house was enveloped in mournful darkness. After hearing a groan at night, Pramath got up from bed. He switched on the bedside lamp and saw that Pratima was sweating profusely. He told Mumpi to look after her and telephoned the Army Hospital. The doctor suggested bringing her to hospital immediately. Pramath lifted her in his arms and took her into the car and drove straight to the hospital. She was wheeled into the ICU, she had suffered from a heart attack, but due to quick and timely operation her life was saved.

Two weeks she was kept in the hospital. Everyday Pramath would visit Pratima in the hospital. She was improving, but at the same time becoming very impatient with him. She had a firm belief that he was not doing enough to rescue Sonai.

"You've killed so many enemies in the Kargil War. Why aren't you killing these terrorists?" she asked him.

She decided that she would not talk with him until he punished the terrorists.

Pramath did not know what to do. He was equally impatient to kill the terrorists, if only he would know their hideouts. At night he would pace on the roof like a caged lion who could take revenge on his enemies at any moment. He would continuously pray to God to show him a way to reach the hideouts of the terrorists.

Ravindar Singh was the new Superintendent of Police of Jalpaiguri district. When the terrorists began a reign of terror and killed half a dozen political leaders, the State Home Minister felt an urgent need to change the top incumbent of the district police. After taking charge, Ravindar called an emergency meeting of the officers of all the police stations. He advised them to revamp the intelligence network, to take the public into confidence, and to interact with the public. The people were both surprised and happy when they saw that the police were participating in their social life and even arranging medical camps.

On the 4th of November, when the terrorists abducted Sonai, but police could not arrest them, Ravindar became very angry. He asked them, "Am

I to believe that all of you are so inefficient? What the hell is our intelligence network doing?" Meanwhile, an informer brought news that cheered up the demoralized police. He gave Ravindar the information that some terrorists were hiding in a village at Kalikhola near the border of Bhutan. Some large arms consignment would arrive in that village and a man named Salem would bring the consignment.

Ravindar ordered his officers to search all the villages near the Indo-Bhutan border, but it was a very difficult task because those villages were located on a rugged hill.

The terrorists hid in a village which was nestled on the slope of a hill that was extremely dense with forest and was on a very high altitude. They were occupying a deserted house on the outskirts of the village and it was on the fringe of that dense forest. People would not visit the house as they would believe it was haunted by a white ghost. The terrorists would hide in the house in the morning and in the evening they would go to the forest to meet the KLO terrorists.

But a little boy chanced to see them in that deserted house. He ran to his home to inform his parents who were surprised when they found that he was panting in great excitement.

His mom asked him, "What's the matter? Why are you panting?" When his breath became normal, words were volleyed out from his mouth: "Mom, dad! Some men have put up in the haunted house," he cried out.

"What nonsense you are talking?" his mom asked anxiously.

He repeated what he had said few moments before. His dad brought photographs of some men that he collected from Jalpaiguri town, where police were handing out those photographs. Now, he asked his son, "Have you seen anyone from these photos?"

"Yes. I've seen this man." The boy pointed to the photograph of Salem.

His mom stopped him hurriedly and told him, "Forget what you have seen. Don't tell anyone whom you have seen in that house. They are very dangerous people. They will kill you if they come to know that you have seen them." But the boy was very courageous.

"Why aren't you informing the police?" he asked his parents.

"We don't want to get into trouble," his mom explained.

The boy was very disappointed when he saw that his parents would not inform the police. He decided to do the task himself. When his parents were sleeping at noon, he fled from home and ran towards the police station. It took him almost five hours of trekking to reach the police station.

At first the constable would not allow him to meet the officer, but he was determined to meet the officer. Hearing noises outside his chamber, the officer came out of his chamber. He told the constable to let the boy come in. The boy told him what he had seen in that haunted house and what his parents told him.

Without wasting any time, the officer telephoned Ravindar, who ordered him to detain the boy until he arrived at the police station. Thereafter, a large posse of police set out for that village.

26

Salem was not inactive during this period. He knew very well that the ISI would not wait to see his blood if he could not make up the loss that his men incurred during the abortive port operation. During his stay in the HuJI-B camp, he was summoned by Khoda Baksh, the same ISI officer, who met the terrorists in a five-star hotel in Kolkata. This time Khoda Baksh summoned him to a secret place in Dhaka. His eyes were blindfolded and two terrorists of the HuJI-B drove him in a black car to a house in a posh locality of Dhaka.

Salem's blood was chilled, looking at the aides of Khoda Baksh. A signal from Khoda Baksh and they could pounce upon him and tear his limbs apart. "Bastard! You've destroyed our vital plan and gifted arms and ammunition worth crores of rupees into the hands of the Indian Security Forces. This is your last chance. If you make any mistake this time, only Allah will know what we do with you!" Khoda Baksh shouted hysterically.

The next two hours Salem listened to the details of the operation he had to execute. He would go to Nepal and cross the border of India. There he would contact the KLO terrorists. In due course of time arms and ammunition would reach them. This time they had to blow up an armoury and a railway station.

A black car was waiting outside Tribhuvan International Airport in Kathmandu. The driver was a staff member of the Pakistani High Commission in Nepal. He handed Salem a fake Nepali passport and a mobile phone. Salem was looking exactly like the person in the passport - a cut mark above the right eyebrow and a mole on the left cheek. His hair was ponytailed and he was looking like a business man.

Though the border was open for the people of both the countries, the officers at the border checkpoint had clear instructions from Delhi to check the passports of those who would enter India. The officer at the border held the passport under the UV rays, but the passport was forged with the latest technique; hence it was impossible to detect that it was a fake one.

Salem cleared the border and headed towards Siliguri. On the way he switched on his mobile phone and contacted the terrorists.

"Hello Mac, this is Roger," he said.

"Hello Roger," answered one terrorist.

"How's the weather today?"

"Clear. Granny is waiting on the top of the hill at Kalikhola."

After the seizure of arms and ammunition and the arrest of Saukat, the intelligence agencies were regularly monitoring every call at the border, particularly at the Nepal border. The operator at the army intelligence department recorded the conversation between Salem and the terrorist, and sent it to the decoding department. They were very excited after decoding the code. They found that Salem had entered India. Immediately, they spotted him and tracked him. Finally, they found his hideout in that remote village on a slope of the hill.

27

"Ahuja! What a pleasant surprise!"

Pramath was astonished when he got the call because only one person would call him Panther, and that was a long time ago. Sam Ahuja and Pramath were batchmates in the National Defence Academy. They were posted in Kashmir and fought together during the Kargil War. Pramath's left shoulder was wounded and thereafter, he accepted early retirement. Ahuja was moved to the army intelligence department and was posted in Fort William. "How are you, buddy?" Ahuja asked.

"Fine, save a little problem," Pramath answered.

"I know it. That's why I've called you. I've information that Salem has come back and this time he has hidden in a house near the Bhutan border.

Our spy satellite has got the picture of the house. It has white windows."

Pramath"s face became stony when he heard the news.

"Well, take care of yourself," Ahuja finished.

Pramath telephoned Boris and said, "I'm going to capture Salem. But I need a friend like you."

Boris was very happy and excited. "Let us name the operation," he suggested.

"Operation White Window will be its name because the house has white windows that we usually see in the UK. A father from the Protestant Church came from the UK and built the house in 1890. He breathed his last in that house," Pramath informed him.

After many years Pramath was feeling the same excitement that he used to feel during the Kargil War. His mind was completely focused on "Operation White Window". He chalked out a detailed plan. Since the terrorists hid on a high slope of the hill, he could not attack them in broad daylight. He had to reach their hiding place at night, climbing the craggy hill for which he was specially trained.

He opened his armory. It held a 7.62 mm bolt-action M600 sniping rifle, which is a cool killing machine, a Beretta Model 87 Cheetah Semi-Auto Pistol 22 LR 3.8 caliber, Czech VZ-52 fighting knife, shot gun, a multi-pronged Swiss knife, two 9 mm pistols, and twenty magazines. The Czech VZ-52 knife was the one he used very deftly to kill enemies in the Kargil War.

Pramath and Boris journeyed in a jeep and drove all day long till they reached Siliguri at dawn. There they checked in a hotel and slept soundly till afternoon. Then they continued the journey again and in the evening they entered the jungle. They hid the jeep with branches and thick foliage. Then they advanced following the trail in the jungle. After an hour's trekking they reached the base of the hill where Salem was hiding. They camped there for the night. Next day before the rooster could crow, they got up and began to climb the hill. As the earth rose towards the hill, the vegetation changed rapidly. Instead of soft yielding soil, they found long outcroppings of rugged stones with deep crevices between them. Pramath was climbing like a panther, leaping from one stone to the other. Boris was not used to such physical strain; so he had to take rest at regular intervals till they reached the top.

The house was surrounded by tall teak trees. Pramath perched on a tree that bent over the back wall of the house. Sitting on a branch, he set his eyes at the telescope of his rifle. The infrared telescope gave a clear picture of the positions of the terrorists inside the house. There were altogether six terrorists in that house. Two were guarding the front part of the house. They were hiding behind the windows at the front side. Two terrorists were positioned at the back door of the house. Salem was sleeping on a bed inside the house and a terrorist was standing beside him.

The terrorists were armed with AK47 rifles and

hand grenades. Pramath watched them for a long time. From long experience he knew pretty well that at dawn those terrorists would feel their eyelids growing heavy and fall to sleep. He got ready to attack them at that time.

At dawn the two terrorists stationed at the back door began to doze. Pramath remembered the key words that he was taught during his training at the National Defence Academy - stealth, speed, surprise. Like a panther he climbed down the wall and walked stealthily towards the terrorists and slashed the soft neck of one terrorist with the knife. Blood gushed forth like water from a spring. The dying terrorist could utter only a soft moan, but it woke up the second one who tried to raise his revolver from his belt, but Pramath slashed his neck very swiftly with the knife. His face was smeared with warm blood. Anyone would have been frightened just looking at him.

Lack of any response from the terrorists from the back door prompted Salem to ask two terrorists to go and check the situation.

By this time Pramath took position at the base of the staircase and Boris cleared the dead bodies behind a tree. One terrorist was coming down the staircase and the other one was covering him. Pramath allowed them to come downstairs. They got alarmed when they did not see their fellows. But it was too late. Pramath did not give them any chance. His Beretta revolver pumped two hot bullets into their hearts and silenced them forever.

Salem was sure that something had gone wrong. He removed his Lugar from the holster and aimed it at the door. He ordered the terrorist to proceed to the door. By this time Pramath and Boris came upstairs. Before the terrorist's forefinger could press the trigger, Pramath shot him twice in the head. The guy collapsed on the ground.

Salem did not waste any time and shot at Pramath from behind the falling terrorist. Pramath felt hot molten lead entering his chest, followed by a heavy pain and then he could not remember anything. When Boris saw that Salem had shot his friend, he fired a couple of rounds at Salem. Salem fell on the ground. He hands and legs were injured, but Boris missed Salem's heart and head.

Meanwhile, Ravindar and his policemen surrounded the house from all sides except the back of the house where there was the dense forest. Through a portable hand mike Ravindar told the terrorists, "We have blocked you from all sides. You have no other choice but to surrender. If you don't come out within five minutes then we will shoot." But nobody came out of the house. Then Ravindar ordered his constables to proceed towards the house.

The front door was locked, but it could not bear the pressure of the heavy boots and soon crumbled. When Ravindar reached the house, he saw Pramath was still alive. He and Boris rushed towards the hospital with the wounded Pramath. Blood had stopped oozing out from the wound, but he was unconscious. Boris was nudging him to bring him back to his senses.

Pramath felt that he plummeted into deep water. .

From far away someone was calling him, but he could not recognize the caller. The white plaster on the walls, the nurses dressed in white aprons, the doctors' anxious faces were vaguely dancing before him. He was lying in the ICU with an oxygen mask and countless wires strapped on his body. A nurse was constantly monitoring his heartbeats on the screen. He could not know his family was standing beside him. Everyone was crying. He did not know that the government had announced that they would reward him with a medal for capturing the terrorist.

Though Pramath was brought to the Army Hospital, and every effort was made to revive him, he succumbed to the wounds. Bikramjeet promised that the police would withdraw their case against Sonai.

The neighbours gathered at the crematorium to pay their last homage to him. Afroj, Boris and Sonai were carrying his dead body. His colleagues came from the barracks. He proved that an Indian soldier always dies like a hero.

The Chief Minister was very happy when he heard the news because he recommended Ravindar's name as the Superintendent of Police. He invited Ravindar in his office to award him for his efficiency and prowess. He asked Ravindar, "Have you come to know who supplied those arms?"

"Salem. He would entrap the innocent youth, luring them with jobs in his fake courier company and through them he would supply arms to the terrorists. Thus he would always remain above suspicion."

Moulavi was sitting before a large Belgium mirror in a closed-door room. A musty smell was wafting in the still air of the room as the room was not inhabited by any human for a long time. In the high power lamp that was shining brightly on the face of Moulavi from the top of the wooden panel of the mirror, he was scrutinizing his face. A small box was laid open before him, arrayed with make-up. He picked up a large tip carefully that he would use as a mole and set it at the corner of his right eye. Next, he opened a bottle of brown dye and poured some drops on a hair brush and then applied it on his thick grey hair, particularly more cautiously on the temples. Finally, he put on specs. He studied his handiwork a long time till he was completely confident that the three terrorists, whom he would be meeting shortly, would not notice anything odd. They had always seen him only in this disguise.

After the make-up was complete, he called them in the house where the RDX was stashed. "Come immediately. It's urgent' he text-messaged them. All of them were recruited from Meerut and Ghaziabad. Like Salem they were also thoroughly brainwashed by him. His modus operandi focused on recruiting youths who didn't have a history of belonging to any terrorist organization. They were simple religious-minded youths whom Moulavi picked from various mosques that they would frequent to attend namaz.

He began the prayer and chose some passages deliberately to keep their morale high. He eyed them thoughtfully. Two of them were mentally strong, but the third one was blinking his eyes. His pathological expression was telling that he was suffering from nervousness.

RDX, which is chemically known as T4, or cyclotrimethylenetrinitramine, is a lethal explosive widely used by the military, but unfortunately the terrorist organizations also use it to make bombs that can cause large-scale destruction when exploded in market places, subways and trains.

They were engaged in making two bombs with RDX and IED (improvised explosive device). Moulavi had a special training for that in the ISI training camp in Karachi.

While making these bombs the terrorists packed them with pellets and embedded micro chips because embedded chips produce a fuse pulse that triggers a detonation. It can be programmed like a digital clock.

After the prayer Moulavi explained that two bombs had to be exploded in any crowded market of Delhi. The purpose was obviously to kill as many people as possible. One bomb would be planted in a car in a shopping complex at Saket and another, in the crowded market at Karol Bagh.

They planned to execute it the next day, but when they watched the television news they felt very alarmed. The news reader was reporting about the consignment at the port of Kidderpore and Afjal's confession.

Moulavi did not waste any time. "Boys, vacate the place at once," he told them.

They hid the bombs in the secret cellar under the house.

Within minutes they left the place.

Moulavi continued to monitor the news. After a week passed he was sure that the police had not got any information about their plan; he still worried that the truck driver who brought the RDX could upset the plan.

He e-mailed Sher Khan informing him about his apprehension.

Nasir Ahmed was very happy after receiving the huge amount for ferrying the mysterious boxes. He wanted to know when he would get the next order. His cousin brother who he met in a safe house of the ISI in Karachi looked at him coldly.

Nasir felt his legs were shaking. He didn't dare ask any question and went back home. After returning from Delhi, he visited a bar and drank like a fish.

The bartender was surprised because Nasir was a frequenter there and he would normally drink three pegs.

"Hey friend, will you be able to pay?" the bartender asked Nasir, who was offended.

He stood up and walked to the bartender. "What do you think? I've no money! Look!" Nasir brought a bunch of five hundred rupee notes from pocket and dangled it before the bartender.

"How have you got so many rupees? Have you robbed any bank?" asked the bartender.

"Who are you to ask me?" Nasir asked angrily.

Nasir was completely sloshed when he left the bar. His legs were staggering. He was singing a popular song. But he did not know his death was waiting for him on the road. A truck was stationed at the side of the road. The driver was sitting at the steering wheel, waiting patiently for his prey.

Nasir was walking, quite oblivious to his surroundings. The road was solitary as it was past midnight. The driver started the engine and drove the truck towards Nasir. The truck hit him with such thrust that he was thrown off the road. The truck fled within seconds and Nasir's mangled body lay on the roadside. Next day a small report was published in a local paper that a man was killed in a truck accident.

When one by one all his operations failed, Sher Khan became very angry. He e-mailed Moulavi to meet him in a hotel in Kathmandu. They discussed about their future plan and finally reached the conclusion that on 25th December they would blast some high explosive devices in New Delhi. The particular date was chosen as it was a festival day and people would throng the multiplexes, markets and restaurants. If they had successfully implemented their plan, a large number of deaths would have been recorded. As a result people would have been frightened and they would curse the government for their inaction against terrorism.

Moulavi called those three terrorists back and explained to them what to do.

In the early morning of Christmas the security was slack at a high-end restaurant at Saket. One or two customers had appeared there for having breakfast. The parking lot was vacant. Two terrorists entered the building in a Mahindra Armada. The terrorist who was at the driver's seat asked the security guard, "Where is the parking lot?"

The guard did not suspect that he was giving space to a deadly car stacked with a bomb. The terrorists parked the car at the farthest corner so that none could spot it at a glance. Then they took the token from the guard and stepped towards the restaurant on the first floor. They ordered two cups of coffee and waited twenty minutes there. Then they got up and strolled out of the building humming tunes so casually that the guard could not guess anything wrong.

Another car was driven by the young terrorist. He was told to leave the car at a crowded place but he was confused about where to park it. After driving madly from one marketplace to another marketplace he steered the car to an open parking space at Karol Bagh, but accidentally pushed another car from behind that got him involved in an altercation with the other car's driver. The altercation continued and by this time some people gathered there.

The terrorist became jittery and suddenly brought out his revolver. It alarmed the people. Some policemen were patrolling nearby. They nabbed him and took him to the police station.

The officer broke into a cold sweat when the terrorist told him where the bombs were planted. The bomb squad was called into action. The restaurant was evacuated immediately. The bomb disposal team entered the parking lot. The security guard never felt so scared in his lifetime when he realised who had come in the morning.

He was thrashed by the officers for not checking the car before allowing it into the parking lot. The timer was on. The captured terrorist disclosed that the bomb would blow up at eleven am. Drops of sweat were streaming down the cheeks of the men of the bomb disposal squad. As the time went by, tension was mounting on everyone. The bomb defusing experts were confused about which wire to cut, as there were two wires- one red and another white. After discussing among themselves, they cut the red one. A grim silence gripped everyone and death danced in each one's eye when they were cutting the wire. At any moment, with the slightest mistake the bomb could go off and the whole area would have been blown up, bringing down the building and killing hundreds of people of the neighbourhood.

There was a breathless pause after the cutting of the red wire; and then everyone realized the bomb was successfully defused; and a sense of relief swept across the security personnel.

The police were not sitting idle. A team immediately set out for Meerut and Ghaziabad in search of the other terrorists. The police artist drew the sketch of their faces according to the description given by the captured terrorist.

Throughout the day the news channels were showing the photos of the three absconding terrorists. Those two who parked the Mahindra Armada at the restaurant's parking lot boarded a train from New Delhi station that was going to Lucknow. By this time many people had seen their photos on television. Some passengers recognized them and began whispering.

The terrorists sensed something was wrong and got down at the next station but by this time a crowd gathered there who began chasing and shouting. The Railway Protection Force members present on the platform took some minutes to understand the situation and began chasing the terrorists. "Drop the guns. You're surrounded from all sides," shouted the RPF personnel, but the terrorists started firing from their revolvers. Two passengers were killed on the spot, and then the RPF officers did not take any chance to catch them alive. They shot them dead.

Another team rushed to the house where RDX was stacked, but Moulavi was not there. He was heading towards Nepal in a car. There, in a hotel in Kathmandu, Sher Khan was waiting for him. He had a very important order to pass on to Moulavi. More RDX and arms had arrived in Nepal and those arms had to be pushed into India. More bomb blasts, more bloodshed, so that India bleeds perennially.

Rajat Kapoor was piecing together all the blocks of the game plan of the ISI to get a rough map of how a nefarious game was planned and almost executed by the ISI, the KLO, and the HuJI-B.

Under tremendous pressure from the US government to crackdown those terrorist groups that were active in Afghanistan, the Pakistani authorities had to take action against those terrorists that obviously proved to be counterproductive as the Frankenstein declared war against its creator. Then the ISI, to divert those terrorists' attention, engaged them to train some pro-Pakistani youths in India, and after training let them sneak into India to carry out subversive activities. It is one of the multi-pronged anti-Indian activities, being perpetrated by the ISI.

But the ISI would never disclose its total plan to its agents. That's why when any captured terrorist would give some information to the Indian intelligence agencies it would bring forward only a partial picture of the game plan of the ISI.

RAW had no information about this mysterious man, Moulavi

Those states that share a common border with Pakistan were put on high alert, but nothing suspicious came to the fore.

The police arrested the leaders of the suspected Indian organizations that had links with the ISI, but they could give no clue. Moulavi was a cunning person who always recruited fresh youths who had no previous police records or were not linked with any organization. His strategy of recruiting only freshers helped him in such situations.

When everything seemed bleak, a ray of hope came from Islamabad. On 24th December Sanjay Basu, the RAW officer of Islamabad High Commission received an e-mail from a Pakistani spy who was on the regular payroll of RAW. The guy wanted to meet Sanjay.

Sanjay decided that he would meet him. A strong cold wind was raging from north. Two spies of the counter espionage department of Pakistan were standing on the main street outside the building, reading newspapers under a lamppost.

Sanjay looked at the mirror in his bedroom till he was satisfied with his make-up. He came out of the house nonchalantly and began walking down the pavement. Two Pakistani spies looked at him and came to the conclusion that he was some plumber who came to do some repair work in the office of the High Commission.

Slowly, Sanjay crossed the road and took a right turn. When they could see him no longer, he took a taxi and told the driver to take him to an address that was on the outskirts of Islamabad. He reached an old house in a dingy slum. The plaster on the façade of the house peeled off. He knocked at the front door. Few minutes later a man opened the door and looked at him suspiciously. Sanjay told him a code word. The man was satisfied and let him in.

They entered the house.

"It's highly risky affair," grunted Sanjay.

"The same is true for me. If they come to know, they will kill me; but this time I can't mail you as the news is very crucial," responded the spy.

"What's the news?" Sanjay asked.

"I've got the name of the man who attempted the serial blasts in your capital," breathed the spy.

"What's his name?" Sanjay asked eagerly.

"He's known as Moulavi and he is the henchman of Sher Khan," answered the man, "and he looks like this."

"So it's Sher Khan's plan to send a consignment of arms to the port of Kidderpore," Sanjay whistled in joy.

"Yes."

"Thank you," said Sanjay, "here is your reward." He slipped a fat packet of dollars in the hand of the spy.

Rajat received this hair-raising information and a sketch of Moulavi from Sanjay at noon of 25th December.

Now, everything was crystal clear to him. The crucial task was to arrest the man. Rajat would know very well that the person would try to sneak out from India. But how would he try it? Certainly, he would not attempt the airports. Then he would try to escape by road. Since the border of Rajasthan, Gujarat, and West Bengal were already sealed, the only option that he would try was to sneak into Nepal.

The intelligence agencies had their officers spread at the Indo-Nepal border in plain-clothes.

Moulavi removed his make-up after sending the terrorists with the car bombs. Then he brought his car from the garage and replaced the number plate with a fake one. He started its engine quickly and was on his way to Nepal. At any cost he had to cross the border because he was definite that Rajat could track him down within twenty-four hours. While leaving Islamabad, he was repeatedly warned by Sher Khan. "Be careful about Rajat because he is the most dangerous person who can upset our plan anytime," Sher Khan said.

"Oh, shit!" those words were volleyed out from Moulavi's mouth when one of the rear side tyres punctured just before crossing the Indo-Nepal border at Jogbani. His plan was to reach Biratnāgar, but this accident upset his plan. He had no jack to change the punctured tyre. The accident took place near a dhaba. Cursing his fate, he started walking towards it.

An old man was sitting behind the counter and some cheap plastic chairs and tables were spread here and there on the vacant lawn in front of the dhaba. Some truck drivers were sitting there, eating bread and some curry. A rustic person was drinking tea. Moulavi went to the counter. The owner greeted him saying, "Namaste sahib."

"Aleyakum," the word came out unconsciously from his mouth, but after saying it, he realised his mistake and looked around to notice if anyone had heard him. Everyone was busy eating or chatting with others. But that rustic fellow heard it. He focused his attention on Moulavi.

"A tyre of my car has punctured," Moulavi told the owner.

He scratched his left ankle with the right leg while talking. The rustic person sat straight. He had precise information that the particular person he was looking for had this typical mannerism. No doubt it was this person all the intelligence agencies were madly after.

The owner of the dhaba called a truck driver and requested him to help Moulavi. When they were talking, that rustic fellow sauntered to the counter, and asked the owner how much he had to pay. With an apathetic look he glanced towards Moulavi and left the place very casually. He acted so naturally that Moulāvi could doubt nothing. When he was out of the sight of the dhaba, he brought a mobile phone from his pocket. He was contacting Rajat.

"Put me to the chief immediately. It's urgent," he told the desk.

Within seconds Rajat received the call.

"Sir, the bird has come into the net," he told Rajat.

"Good, stay there. I'm sending forces immediately," Rajat replied.

The truck driver and his assistant were still engaged in fitting a new tyre to the car. Moulavi was standing beside them and anxiously looking at his wristwatch.

At first he noticed a number of jeeps were heading towards him kicking up a storm of dust from the road. He understood who they were. With the swiftness of a panther, he jumped behind a truck that was parked near his own car. The jeeps screeched to a halt few yards away from the car and the commandos jumped out from the jeeps and took positions. They spread in different directions to block the escape route of Moulavi. Seeing so many commandos, the owner and other people had no doubt that the man was a notorious terrorist. Terrified, they hid inside the dhaba.

The first bullet Moulavi fired towards a commando who was inching towards him from the left side hit the commando's bullet proof jacket. Next half-hour a rain of bullets sprayed from all sides.

Moulavi wanted to get on the truck; hence he tried to spray the commandos with bullets so that he could keep them at bay, but quick shots from the commandos flattened the tyres of his car. A commando threw shells of tear gas in quick succession. They had clear instructions to capture Moulavi alive. The shells burst under the truck and tear gas was released that created a smoke screen. Moulavi could not fight any more and fell down choking.

When he was being taken to the jeep, his mobile phone began ringing. Rajat picked the phone from Moulavi's trouser pocket. Rajat's face was radiant with a bright smile when he looked at the screen of the mobile. "Look! Who has been calling you?" he told Moulavi, who saw Sher Khan was calling him. He cast a baleful look at Rajat and scuffled with the commandos, but they thrust him into a jeep. Rajat received the call and said, "Hello".

Sher Khan understood that it was not Moulavi's voice; he kept silent for few seconds and then asked, "Who's it?"

"Glad to talk to you, Sher Khan. I'm Rajat Kapoor. Bangladesh War!" Rajat told him testily.

"Where is he?" Sher Khan asked angrily.

"Don't worry; he's perfectly all right in our custody. Now, you see your game is over," Rajat answered.

Sher Khan threw the mobile phone at the looking glass in the hotel room in utter frustration. The glass broke with a piercing sound.

A commando advanced to Rajat and asked, "Sir, shall we go after him?"

"We can't because he is enjoying a diplomat's privilege," replied Rajat.

Sher Khan had already headed towards Kathmandu Airport to leave for Islamabad.

After Pramath's death Pratima requested Mumpi to marry Afroj as soon as possible. Pramath always wanted it because he liked Afroj very much. Hence one day she invited Afroj round for tea.

Afroj would work in an NGO whose function was rehabilitating HIV positive street children. The organization would work under the umbrella of the Global Fund to Fight Aids, Malaria, and T.B. (GFFAMT). Two years ago he mooted the idea of such a rehabilitation centre. The authorities of the GFFAMT in London accepted the concept and told Afroj to prepare a pilot project. Two days later the chief of the GFFAMT was scheduled to come to Kolkata to inaugurate the project.

Afroj told Mumpi, "I wish you would come with me. My colleagues are very eager to meet you."

"I'll tell you my decision in the morning," she replied. He was very upset because nowadays she was avoiding him on petty pretexts. He noticed that she had been doing this after the release of Sonai.

Next day he got up very early in the morning. Then he made a cup of tea and sat at the window, slowly sipping tea. He was waiting for her phone call.

He remembered how after the death of his mother he sold off the house and settled down here. He lived in an old house in a dingy lane, which was hardly two hundred feet long, and three feet wide; yet fifty houses stood like match boxes in that stifling space.

Only Mumpi knew that he had faced a grim tragedy in his life. His dad was a mason. One day his dad told his mom, "I've decided to go to Saudi Arab. There dollars fly in the air. If I can catch them, we'll become rich." Afroj's mom did not like the idea, but did not prevent him either.

So his dad flew to Saudi Arab. He bribed a tout twenty thousand bucks for a passport, a visa, and a job. Six months later Afroj's mom got some money and a letter. His dad wrote in the letter, "I've got a job in a construction company. From now on I'll send you money." One year later they purchased a house. Afroj got admission in a local English medium school. His dad would come home once in a year, but each time he would bring lots of gifts for them.

When Afroj was eighteen years old, his dad returned from Saudi Arab permanently. They were very happy when he told them that he would not return to Saudi Arab, but he did not disclose to them that he was suffering from AIDS. During the long separation from his wife, he used to visit the brothels, where he caught the lethal disease. The construction company where he worked would carry out regular blood tests for all of its employees. When the company came to know that he was an AIDS patient, they sent him home. At first Afroj and his mother did not know it, but gradually the disease revealed its symptoms - often he would have fever.

Afroj took him to a doctor's. Observing the symptoms, the doctor prescribed for HIV tests. The day Afroj went to collect the reports from the clinic, his dad committed suicide on the railway tracks. His mom could not survive the blow, and very soon she followed her husband to the grave.

Afroj became alone in the world. He did not know what to do. He felt as if he had lost his passion for life, and he was on the verge of mental depression. At that time he saw a TV programme on AIDS. An NGO was conducting a seminar on AIDS. A man was saying, "India is the global centre for this Pandemic…the Indian epidemic is on African trajectory…and the future will be like Botswana and South Africa. Given the presence of tuberculosis and other infections in India, the progress from HIV to full-blown AIDS will be faster in India than in the West."

At that time he decided that he would join this NGO. For that he had to undergo a special medical training before he could take care of those poor children. He learnt how to treat those children for ailments like fever, cough, and cold. His dedication moved his colleagues.

After the death of his parents, he clung to Mumpi like a traveller who clings to an oasis in a desert. Although they belonged to different religions, it never get in the way of their love. Yet obstacles came from outside. The mullas propagated that he was making love with an infidel. They decreed a fatwa that he must forsake her, but he told them in clear terms to mind their own business.

His dream-like state was shattered by a phone call. It was Mumpi. She was telling him, "I'm sorry Afroj, but I can't attend the party."

"Why can't you come with me?" his voice was twisted in pain.

"I've a nasty headache. Please excuse me," she replied trying utmost to conceal her sorrow. Her voice was very dry.

But her explanation could not convince him.

The Taj Bengal's ballroom was hired for the party. His colleagues were asking him about her absence. He felt embarrassed because he had promised them that he would bring her to the party. His best friend Aman guessed that something was wrong. He rescued him from the awkward questions and took him aside.

"Anything wrong?" he wanted to know.

"She is changed. But believe me, I don't know why?" Afroj looked very helpless.

"Better you ask her," Aman advised him.

Mumpi was sleepless that night. Time and again his words were drifting towards her mind. Remembering that, she was crying silently. How could she reveal that she was fraught with such a pain that neither she could bear nor share. He wished that she would go with him to the party, but she had avoided it because she feared that he might announce their wedding date in the party.

Next day, when she was entering her office, she saw that he was waiting for her at the entrance of the office.

Drawing a pale smile on her face she asked him, "How long?"

"I want to talk to you. Can we sit in the café we used to go?"

Inside the café he asked her, "What's the matter? Why did you not come with me? Why are you avoiding me?"

The last words he said so loudly that other visitors of the café looked at them curiously.

"I can't marry you, Afro," she said finally.

Returning home, she chatted with her mother for a long time. Then she went to her bedroom. Before going to bed, she rang up Afroj and told him, "I'm so sorry for breaking your heart. Please forgive me."

Then she took out some strips of sleeping pills

from the drawer, and popped them and drifted into sleep.

When she woke up, she saw that she was lying on a bed in a hospital.

"Why did you do it?" Pratima asked her.

"Oh, mom! I can't tell you. You don't know that I've betrayed Afroj. When Sonai was kidnapped by the terrorists, I began to feel that I was the cause of his plight. When the lawyer said that his life was hanging on the statement of Santanu, I made up my mind. I gave in myself to fulfill his lust. But I have lost Afroj forever, mom!" She sobbed her heart out.

"Oh, my dear! You have sacrificed yourself for your brother. I wish I could touch your feet. But there are certain things in our life that we must keep as a secret; even from our beloved. You know what I mean," Pratima told her.

She embraced Mumpi and held her close to her heart.

31

Sonali was nine months' pregnant when Sonai was abducted. The gynaecologist who treated her said that the baby was in a normal condition and there was nothing to worry. Naturally, she and Boris were very happy. The day Boris went with Pramath on the mission, she fell on the toilet floor and suffered a miscarriage.

She accused Boris of negligence to her and her baby, and left home.

The telephone was ringing continuously. Sonali could hear it, but didn't care to pick it up. She was lazing on the bed. Mitali had gone to the market. Niraud was reading a newspaper in the living room. He ambled into the bedroom to pick up the phone. He knew who it would be. Hence when Boris requested him to give the call to Sonali, he had to tell him the lie that she was not at home.

When Niraud was talking to him, Sonali left the room. She was least interested to listen to Boris. After that tragic incident, she deserted him and came to her parents' house. Few minutes later Niraud joined her on the roof. "Can you remember that you and I planted this creeper beside the septic tank? Last time when you visited it, you put a ladder on the wall and placed it on the ladder. Now, it has climbed the whole way to the roof," he told her.

She trudged to the side of the roof and touched the tender leaves of the creeper. Yes, she could remember. She touched its leaves that aroused tender feelings inside her heart. As if a flow of milk was oozing from her breasts. Suddenly, a few drops of tears fell from her eyes on a leaf.

After the accident she passed through a trauma - often she would get startled looking at her image in the mirror - a murderer's image would come up; sometimes the photo of a cute baby.

Towards the evening a greyish cloud began to spread at the horizon and behind it a storm was waiting to loom heavily across the Earth. Continuous lightning flashed across the sky setting the sky ablaze and an ominous thunder was rolling from the horizon that scared the homecoming ravens and sparrows. The poor birds were circling aimlessly under the dark cloud, not knowing how to return home.

A grey blanket of dust rose over the mango garden, and the earth, heavy with the unbearable heat of summer, was trembling at the prospect of a mad shower which would sweep off all the dirt from her feet. Within an hour rain came down heavily blurring the vision of the setting sun, the sky, the trees and the birds. Mitali was calling them to come downstairs but she was not in a frame of mind to respond to the call. Her whole existence wanted to be a part of the tumultuous nature. She stood like a tree, holding both arms heavenwards - rainwater was running down her body like flood. Rain ruffled the pent up emotions inside her; during that time she stood still in a trance. When the rain stopped, she felt that all her sufferings were swept away by the rain.

The house stood between two ponds. Many years ago a thunder blighted a coconut tree. Niraud chopped the tree and placed two logs on the thresholds to connect those two ponds. Sonali changed her clothing and sat on a threshold. Some frogs were croaking from behind some shrubs near a pond. Mitali broke the silence. "We will settle at Bibeknagar, selling the house. You live there. Who'll look after us in our old age?"

"You're starting that nonsense again," Niraud scolded her.

Sonali could not tell her that she would never return to Boris.

"Dear Sonali, I know very well how much pain you'd undergone after the tragedy, but believe me, I was no less afflicted. You've accused me of negligence to you, but haven't I given you all those things that a wife expects from her husband. I'd always tried to protect you, care about you, give you love. You asked me why I went to Bhutan with Pramath, but what I could do when he was in great trouble- the life of his son was in great danger! You knew it very well.

I know you wove a dream and cherished it for a long time, but I had also shared your dream. In fact we started a journey together and we should continue it till we die.

Mutual love, respect and trust that once would prevail in our relation are now replaced by mistrust.

I urge you to uproot the mistrust from your mind because it's a malady that vitiates your mind and you'll not find any peace in mind.

I do believe that one day you'll understand me and come back to me. Until then I'll wait for you."

Boris posted the letter to Sonali.

Then he went to the bank of the river beside the wharf. He chose a solitary place. At that time the wharf was busy ferrying people. But he was completely detached from the outside world. He shut his perception of the surroundings. He was completely within himself. He was thinking something deeply. At eleven o'clock at night, after the last boat left the wharf, the man who was giving tickets to the passengers shut down the counter. He was ready to go home. He noticed that Boris was sitting on the bank.

"Sir, won't you go home?" he asked Boris.

"What's the time now," Boris asked slowly. He was least interested in going back home.

Boris decided that he would start his life afresh which was an effort to move the wheel of time backward; but he knew how difficult it would be. Many years ago there was a banyan tree in their garden. He was a mere child at that time. The tree was surrounded by some small saplings. He would call those tiny plants the sons of the banyan tree. When he was six years old, his father sent him to a boarding school. After that he forgot all about them. After completing his twelfth grade, he came back home and was admitted into a college. One day he came to that garden to collect some flowers. To his amazement he saw that the old banyan tree was dead, standing beside the gravel-strewn-garden path like a cursed person - its branches were black, dry and curled up. But those saplings that he would fondly call the sons of the banyan tree were standing firm and robust.

He bequeathed all his property to Sonai. Next day he went to the orphanage very early in the morning.

He entered the room where the pyre of the sadhu baba was kept. The boarders were surprised to see him so early in the morning. Boris asked them, "Where is that tiny child whom Pramath brought from the terrorists' camp?"

He had come for the child- his last hope.

He thought, "Only this child can rescue me from the pain. I must rekindle my lost idealism through this boy. I'll bring him up. I'll prove to myself that I'm not defeated. There is always space to turn around."

The will created a stir in the house. Sonai went to meet Boris. He noticed that the door of his bedroom was open and the bed was tidy, which suggested that he did not lie on it last night. He was surprised.

"Where has he gone so early in the morning?" he asked himself.

Sonai waited there till afternoon. When the sun went down but he did not return, Sonai felt worried. He looked around the bedroom. This time he found another letter under the pillow. After reading it he came to know that Boris had gone to the orphanage. He told Pratima. They went there to meet him.

At the orphanage Pratima saw that Boris was playing with the children. She asked him, "What do you think? You can forsake us? You're a selfish fellow." She began to cry.

"Please don't cry. We've spent many wonderful years in joy and sorrow. I'll never forget Pramath and you. But I'll never return home," Boris replied.

"If it is your final decision, then I've nothing to say." She left the place.

Boris informed the Home authorities that he wanted to adopt the child. They told him, "We need time before giving permission." Boris expected that his decision would make them happy. He was a bit upset, but waited patiently.

An hour later they told him that they would be happy to give him permission to adopt the child but he had to fulfill some legal formalities that might require few months. He thanked them. Before leaving the orphanage, he looked at it for the last time. The building - its walls, windows, doors, the garden, the pond- was now beginning to be just a blur for him. The boys were running in the playground. He stretched his hands to touch them, but...he would not know whether he was doing right or wrong. For the last time he looked at the building with all his love and affection.

Four months later a Jet Airways' airbus touched Heathrow early in the morning. The sky was foggy; a mild cold wind was tickling the skin. The child was sleeping on his lap. Looking at his face Boris felt a strange fatherly emotion. Exiting the plane, Boris followed the other passengers who were briskly moving on the long escalators. The child was on his shoulder. At the end of those escalators there were long queues. Some airport officials were crying out "First time students!"

The single line was soon divided into three: one for EU passengers, one for students, one for non-EU passengers. The third queue was the longest and it stretched a long way in a serpentine manner. His mobile phone had been switched off on the plane. As soon as he switched it on, it began ringing frantically. Pratima was calling him from India.

"Why is your phone off? I am so anxious," she asked.

"Everything is fine. We've just landed. We are now in the airport," he assured her.

Uncle Ned had informed him that there was a coach service between Heathrow and Victoria, which was cheap and comfortable. He also read on the website that the route was underground, but he could not find it out. He asked a police officer who showed him the underground route. An hour later they arrived at Victoria Coach Station.

A gentleman was coming down the Buckingham Palace road. He was carrying an umbrella in one hand and an office bag in the other. He stopped before them and said smilingly, "My dear, you seem to be lost!"

"I'm looking for a pub at Soho, but I can't find the road," Boris replied.

The gentleman showed him the route with a sketch on a piece of paper.

He stopped at the crossing of Buckingham Palace Road and Victoria Street, and opened the map. He turned left and crossed Buckingham Road, then took a left at the next crossing at Bank of Scotland, and finally arrived at Grosvenor Road. The road led him up to Hyde Park. He noticed a subway; some people were entering it. He also entered it.

When he finally reached Soho, he was

heartened to see Ned, Sheila and Morris standing at the door of the pub to welcome his son and him into a new life.